통조림 공장

아시아에서는 《바이링궐 에디션 한국 대표 소설》을 기획하여 한국의 우수한 문학을 주제별로 엄선해 국내외 독자들에게 소개합니다. 이 기획은 국내외 우수한 번역가들이 참여하여 원작의 품격을 최대한 살렸습니다. 문학을 통해 아시아의 정체성과 가치를 살피는 데 주력해 온 아시아는 한국인의 삶을 넓고 깊게 이해하는 데 이 기획이 기여하기를 기대합니다.

Asia Publishers presents some of the very best modern Korean literature to readers worldwide through its new Korean literature series 〈Bilingual Edition Modern Korean Literature〉. We are proud and happy to offer it in the most authoritative translation by renowned translators of Korean literature. We hope that this series helps to build solid bridges between citizens of the world and Koreans through a rich in-depth understanding of Korea.

바이링궐 에디션 한국 대표 소설 068

Bi-lingual Edition Modern Korean Literature 068

The Canning Factory

편혜영
통조림 공장

Pyun Hye-young

ASIA
PUBLISHERS

Contents

통조림 공장

The Canning Factory

공장장이 출근하지 않았다는 얘기는 순식간에 퍼졌다. 첫 번째 결근이었다. 눈치 빠른 사람들은 무슨 일인가 생긴 게 틀림없다고 생각했다. 공장장은 직원들 중 가장 먼저 출근했고 가장 늦게 퇴근했다. 누군가 공장장이 아니라 수위 같다고 빈정거렸고 그 후 공장장은 직원들 사이에서 수위로 불렸다. 그는 공장이 자동화되기 이전의 생산직 출신이었다. 그 무렵 근로자들이 대부분 그렇듯이, 그 역시 기계 덕을 보면서도 기계를 잘 믿지 못했다. 녹 검사부터 진공도 검사까지, 제조 후 표본 검사 수를 두 배로 올렸다. 그러면서도 기계가 일을 다 하고 있어 직원들이 멍하니 빈 깡통을 보며 시간을

Word spread instantly that the plant manager had not come in to work that day. It was his first absence without notice. The quick ones were positive that something was wrong. The plant manager was always the first to report to work and the last to leave. After someone once joked that he was more of a security guard than a plant manager, Security Guard became his code name amongst the employees. He started out at the factory in the production line before automation happened. As did most of the workers at the time, he couldn't trust the new machines, even if they simplified things. From rust inspections and vacuum degree tests to

때운다고 틈만 나면 잔소리를 퍼부었다. 업무 방식을 일일이 지시하는 식으로 모든 공정에 간섭했다. 명찰을 똑바로 달라며 비뚤어진 명찰이 달린 가슴께에 손을 갖다대 여직원들을 질겁하게 했고 그런 후에는 가슴의 크기를 가지고 노골적인 음담패설을 퍼부어 모욕을 주었다. 성격이 급해서 잘잘못을 따지기 전에 화부터 냈고 자신의 오해이거나 실수임이 밝혀진 후에도 사과하지 않았다. 공장장의 결근 원인을 확인하느라 사장이 직원들을 면담하는 과정에서 나온 말이었다. 온전히 믿을 수는 없었다. 공장장이란 늘 평판이 나쁜 법이었다.

전날 함께 야근을 했던 박의 말에 따르면 공장장은 술을 한잔 하자는 요청을 박이 거절하자 요즘 젊은 것들은 제멋대로라는 비난을 퍼붓고는 사택 쪽으로 걸어갔다.

술 취해서 뻗은 거 아니야?

사장이 박에게 물었다. 그렇게 묻기는 했지만 그럴 리 없다는 걸 잘 알았다. 공장장은 거의 매일 술을 마셨고 취했으나 다음 날이면 어김없이 술냄새와 함께 가장 먼저 출근해 있었다. 말하자면 그는 성실한 알코올중독자였다. 박은 고개를 갸우뚱거릴 뿐 대답하지 않았다.

post-manufacture sampling, the new machines doubled performance. Still, he nagged at the workers every chance he could for letting the machines do all the work while they passed the time staring at empty cans. He was the micro-managing type, intervening in everything the employees did. He insisted that name badges be pinned straight, alarming female employees when he touched the crooked badges on their chest. Then, he would blatantly make dirty comments about their chest size. He was quick-tempered and didn't care to distinguish right from wrong. He never apologized, even when it was clear that he was mistaken or at fault. This was how the employees described the plant manager to the company president, who had met with them to figure out the reason behind his absence. But they couldn't all be taken at face value. Plant managers always had bad reputations.

According to Park, who had worked overtime with the plant manager the night before, the manager had asked to go out for a drink with him. When Park declined, he criticized today's young people for doing as they pleased and started to walk home.

"Maybe he just passed out after a night of drink-

그런데 어제는 무슨 일로 야근을 했나?

야근을 해야 할 만큼 바쁠 리 없었다. 공장 직원들은 대도시 기업체의 사무원도 지키지 못하는 9시 출근, 6시 퇴근을 준수하고 있었다. 듣기에 불황은 세계적인 추세라고 했다. 가공식품의 위생을 의심하는 목소리는 나날이 높아졌다. 잊을만하면 통조림에서 이물질이, 그러니까 칼날이나 파리나 구두충이나 비닐 같은 것이, 심지어는 손톱의 일부가 발견되었다. 뉴스에 보도가 나갈 때마다 매출이 곤두박질쳤다. 국내 납품 물량이 줄었다. 수출로 명맥을 유지하고 있지만 인접국의 저가 공략에 맥을 못 췄다.

공장장님의 개인적인 부탁이었습니다.

박이 대답했다.

개인적인 부탁이라고?

사장이 말을 이었다.

자네가 잊어버렸나 본데, 여긴 공장이야. 개인적인 일로는 수당을 주지 않아.

통조림을 만들었습니다.

말이 떨어지기 무섭게 박이 대답했다.

하하, 그럼 내가 내 공장에서 뭘 만들었다고 생각하는

ing?" the president suggested.

But he knew how unlikely that was. The manager got drunk nearly every night, but always managed to appear—reeking of alcohol—first at work the very next morning. A diligent alcoholic, if you will. Park tilted his head but gave no reply.

"Why'd you have to work overtime yesterday anyway?"

The factory was not busy enough to require overtime work. The employees abided by the nine to six workday—something that big city office workers dreamed of. They heard that the recession was global. Suspicions about the sanitation of processed foods grew each day. And just when the last incident was forgotten, they'd find something in the canned food. Something like a knife blade or a fly or a spiny-headed worm or a piece of plastic, even a broken fingernail once. News reports of such incidents were always followed by a plunge in sales. Domestic shipments fell. Exports barely kept the company afloat due to the low-cost strategies of neighboring countries.

"It was a personal favor for the manager," Park replied.

"A personal favor?"

줄 안 거야? 여기서는 통조림만 만들어. 어제도 그제도 그랬고 23년 전에도 그랬지. 오늘도 내일도 그럴 거야. 23년 후에도 그럴 거고.

T국으로 보낸다고 했습니다.

그런 수출 물량이 있는지 생각하는 눈빛으로 사장이 박을 빤히 쳐다보았다.

T국?

공장장님 딸이 T국에서 연수 중입니다.

그랬단 말이군.

사장이 고개를 끄덕였다.

박은 사장이 뭔가 쥐고 있었다면 깨뜨릴 것처럼 손에 힘을 주는 걸 지켜보았다.

공장장놈, 잘도 배웠어.

사장이 중얼거렸다.

자식에게 보낼 통조림이라면 어떤 것인지 잘 알았다. 사장은 오래전 아들 녀석이 U국에서 유학을 할 당시, 정기적으로 통조림에 음식을 밀봉하여 보낸 적이 있었다. 갓 담근 김치와 잘 익은 깍두기를, 간장에 자박자박 담근 게장과 조리기만 하면 되는 양념갈비와 불고기, 낙지볶음 같은 것을 깡통에 담았다. 식혜를, 김치찌개

The president continued.

"Perhaps you've forgotten, but this is a factory. There's no pay for personal business."

"I canned food," blurted Park.

"Hah! What else would you make in my factory? We only make canned food here. That's what we made yesterday, and the day before that, and 23 years ago. That's what we're making today, tomorrow, and what we'll be making 23 years from now, too."

"He said he was shipping it to Country T."

The president gave Park a look that suggested he wasn't sure whether the company made shipments there.

"Country T?"

"His daughter is studying there."

"So I see."

The president nodded. Park kept his eyes on the president's fist, clenched so tight it looked to be crushing something.

"That little plant manager... I guess he sure did learn something..." he muttered.

The president knew well what foods were good to send to children abroad. When his own son was studying abroad in Country U back in the day, he

를, 아욱된장국을, 볶은 멸치를 밀봉했다. 유학을 하는 동안 아들이 음식 때문에 고생하는 일은 없었다. 그 일을 해준 것이 공장장이었다. 그렇긴 해도 사장도 아닌 주제에 생산과 상관없이 기계를 돌리고 전력을 소모하고 업무가 끝난 후에 직원을 부려먹었다는 거였다. 화가 난 사장은, 걱정이 되어 공장장이 묵는 사택에 박을 보내려던 생각을 거뒀다. 공장장은 독신자용 사택에서 혼자 지냈다. 부인은 어학연수 중인 딸을 돌보러 T국에 가 있었다. 다음 날에도 그다음 날에도 공장장은 나타나지 않았다. 사장은 다시는 공장에 발도 못 붙이게 하겠다며 비서를 겸하는 총무과장을 사택으로 보냈다. 해고 사실을 알리기 위해서였다.

점심을 먹으러 각 구역 휴게실에 모인 직원들은 꽁치와 고등어, 양념깻잎 통조림 뚜껑을 따고 집에서 싸온 말간 쌀밥을 꺼냈다.

이건 수위 스타일이 아니야.

직원 중 하나가 꽁치를 씹으며 말했다. 공장장 스타일이라면 아파서 당장 죽을 지경이더라도 술냄새를 풍기며 제일 먼저 공장에 나와 있어야 했다. 누군가 별일이야 있겠느냐고 했다가 그래도 경찰에 신고해야 하는 게

periodically canned food to ship to him. Freshly-made *kimchi*, well-fermented *kkakdugi* (cubed radish), raw crabs stacked in soy sauce brine, ready-to-cook marinated *galbi* ribs and *bulgogi*. He canned spicy stir-fried octopus. He sealed *sikhye* (sweet rice drink), *kimchi* stew, soup made with soybean paste and curled mallow, and seasoned anchovies. At least his son didn't have to worry about food while he was away from home. It was the plant manager who had done all the canning for him. Regardless, he had run the machines, used up electricity, and had asked an employee to come in after hours—all for something unrelated to production and as an employee, not the president. The president, now angry, had changed his mind about sending Park to check on him at his residence. He lived alone at a company housing arrangement for singles; his wife was with their daughter in Country T. He hadn't shown up the next day, nor the day after that. Bent on not allowing him to set foot on the factory grounds again, the president sent the general affairs manager to his residence. He was firing him.

At lunchtime, the factory workers gathered at their respective rest lounges, opened cans of Pa-

아닐까 말했고 동의하듯 다들 꽁치나 고등어, 깻잎 중 하나를 밥과 함께 씹으며 고개를 끄덕였다.

이걸 보니 수위 생각이 나.

누군가 뚜껑을 딴 통조림을 가리켰다. 공장장은 아침에는 혼자 사택에서, 점심에는 직원들과 함께 휴게실에서 통조림을 반찬 삼아 밥을 먹었다. 저녁에는 통조림을 안주로 술을 마셨다.

왜 그러고 살았대?

누군가 깻잎에 흰 쌀밥을 말아 입에 넣고 우물우물 씹으며 물었다.

누군 안 그러고 사나?

밥을 씹으며 누군가 대꾸했다. 대답에서 비린 고등어 냄새가 풍겼다. 모두들 잠자코 국물이 스민 밥을 꽁치나 고등어 살점과 함께 입에 떠 넣었다. 유난히 천천히 밥을 씹었다. 모두들 약간의 시차를 두고 공장장의 일과와 식사가 자신들과 다르지 않다는 걸 깨달았다. 열심히 일했고 고분고분 살았지만, 어쩌면 그래서인지도 모르지만, 씹고 있는 통조림의 맛처럼 삶이 너무 자명해진 느낌이었다. 미래는 아직 시작되지도 않았는데 이미 지나버린 것 같았다. 지나버린 미래는 공장장의 현

cific saury, blue mackerel, and pickled perilla leaves, and took out containers of white rice they had brought from home.

"This is not like Security Guard," commented one of the workers while chewing some saury. Even if he were dying, the plant manager would've been the first one at the factory, reeking of alcohol but present nonetheless. Someone else remarked that it was probably nothing serious, while another suggested he should probably have been reported to the police as missing. As if in agreement, everyone took a bite of rice with either their saury, mackerel or perilla leaves, and nodded their heads.

"All this reminds me of him."

Someone pointed at the opened cans. The plant manager ate canned food for breakfast alone at the residence, and canned food for lunch in the lounge with employees. In the evenings, he had canned food with his alcohol.

"How does he live like that?" someone else asked. He wrapped a perilla leaf over some rice and popped it in his mouth.

"Who doesn't?" responded yet another worker, his mouth full of food. The deep, salty smell of mackerel accompanied his response. In silence,

재와 다름없을 거였다. 그것도 믿고 싶지는 않지만 아주 성공적일 경우에만. 공장장이 싫었지만 딱히 미워할 수 없는 게 그 때문이었다. 딱히 그럴 이유가 없는데 공장장이 싫은 것도 그 때문이었다.

밥을 다 먹은 후에는 복숭아와 감귤 통조림을 후식으로 먹었다. 말랑말랑한 복숭아 과육을 씹으며 누가 경찰에 전화를 할 것인지 논의했다. 그러면서 힐끔 박의 눈치를 살폈다. 아무래도 마지막으로 만난 사람이니까 혹시 공장장에게 모두가 짐작하고 있는 것처럼 나쁜 일이 생긴 거라면, 그때쯤에는 누구나 분명 무슨 일이 생긴 게 틀림없다고 생각하고 있었는데, 박이 곤란을 겪지 않을까 해서였다. 하지만 박에게는 알리바이가 있었다. 박은 야간 근무를 끝내고 저녁을 먹기 위해 단골 식당에 들렀다. 식당에는 같은 공장 동료가 저녁을 먹고 있었다. 박은 우연히 만난 동료와 합석했다. 마침 텔레비전에서는 근래 가장 시청률이 높은 드라마가 방영되고 있었다. 박은 여자 주인공이 왜 계속 목에 힘줄이 다 보이도록 악다구니를 쓰는지 음식을 내준 식당 주인에게 물었다. 식당 주인은 여자 주인공을 대신해 하소연하듯 사정을 늘어놓았다. 최후 행적의 목격자라고 해서

they placed chunks of saury or mackerel atop their rice, which by this point was flavored with juices from the cans. They spooned it all in and chewed slowly. Everyone came to realize that the manager's daily routine, including his meals, were not too different from their own. They worked hard and lived submissively, and perhaps that's why, similar to the taste of canned food in their mouths, the direction of their lives had become all too blunt and obvious. The future had yet to begin, but it was as though it had already passed. The manager's present would be their long gone future. And if that wasn't hard enough to accept, this would only be the case for a successful few. That also explained why they disliked him for no particular reason.

To finish off lunch, they ate canned peaches and canned mandarins. They nibbled on the plump peach slices and discussed who would call the police, stealing glances at Park when they could. He had been, in fact, the last one to see the manager, and if something bad *did* happen as everyone suspected—and by that time everyone was sure something had happened—Park would be in a sticky situation. But Park had an alibi. After work that night, he had gone to his usual diner for a bite

박이 의심을 받을 건 없었다. 술에 취해 돌아가다가 실족해 다리 아래로 굴러 운 나쁘게 강에 빠지거나 괴한에게 지갑을 뺏기고 죽을 지경이 되도록 폭행을 당하거나 뺑소니 차량에 치여 알 수 없는 곳에 버려지는 사고는 얼마든지 있었고 누구든지 당할 수 있었다.

누군가 마지막 남은 복숭아를 입에 넣으려고 할 때 총무과장이 휴게실로 달려왔다. 그는 숨을 고르고 나서 먼저 복숭아 통조림 당액을 들이켰다.

그렇게 마시다가 입술 베요.

깡통째 들고 마시는 총무과장에게 누군가 말했다.

내가 이걸 하루 이틀 먹냐? 어제도 먹고 그제도 먹고 12년 전에도 먹었는데.

총무과장이 깡통을 내려놓으며 말했다.

사장이 경찰에 실종 신고를 했어.

모두들 뚜껑을 잘못 딴 깡통에 입술이라도 벤 듯 짧게 탄식을 내뱉었다.

그랬더니 경찰이, 총무과장이 복숭아 통조림의 당액을 마저 들이마셨다. 누군가 그의 말을 기다리며 침을 꿀꺽 삼켰다. 단순 가출일지도 모르니 더 기다려보라고 했대.

to eat when he spotted a co-worker and joined him. The latest hit TV drama series happened to be airing. As the owner of the diner brought out his order, Park asked how the main character could be so ill-willed that the veins in her neck looked like they were about to burst. The owner started to give a long defense on the main character's behalf. Park could not have been a witness of the manager's final whereabouts. Drunk, he could have tripped on his way home, rolled down a hill under a bridge, and drowned in the river. Someone could have attacked him and ran away with his wallet after beating him to death. He could have even been hit by a car and dragged off to an unknown location. Anyone could be subject to such accidents.

Just as the last peach slice was about to disappear the general affairs manager came rushing into the lounge. He caught his breath and drank the peach syrup straight from the can.

"You'll cut your lip that way," someone said.

"You think I haven't done this before? I did it yesterday and the day before that. Heck, twelve years ago, even."

The general affairs manager put the can down.

"The president reported him as missing to the

그는 말이 끝나자 이번에는 감귤 통조림의 당액을 들이마셨다. 한데서 추위에 떨다 따뜻한 어묵 국물을 먹고 몸을 녹이듯 직원들은 통에 든 당액을 조금씩 나눠 마셨다. 아무도 입술을 베지 않았다. 마지막 국물을 들이마신 이가 뚜껑을 벌린 빈 깡통을 모아 들었다. 깡통끼리 부딪치는 소리가 작게 들렸고 그게 신호인 듯 점심시간이 끝났음을 알리는 종이 울렸다.

*

박은 꽁치 통조림 밀봉 담당이었다. 실종된 공장장이 막 임명되었을 당시 잠시 고등어 통조림을 만들기도 했지만 그때를 제외하면 내내 꽁치 통조림만 만들었다. 담당은 마음껏 바꿀 수 있었다. 비릿하고 짠내에 속이 메슥거린다면 농산물 라인으로 옮겨 복숭아나 감귤 통조림을 만들 수 있었다. 계속되는 단내에 현기증이 날 정도라면 다시 수산물 라인으로 옮기면 되었다. 원칙은 그랬지만 누구도 담당을 바꾸지 않았다. 교체를 자유롭게 한 것은 공장장이었다. 그는 입사 후 12년간 줄곧 꽁치 통조림만 만들었다. 공장 설립 초기였다. 나중에는

police."

They gasped, as if someone had cut his lip on a poorly opened can.

"The police said—" The manager downed the rest of the syrup. Someone gulped while waiting for him to finish. "—He could've just run away, so they said we should just wait and see."

He picked up the mandarin can and drank. They took turns drinking the rest of the cans like they were drinking hot fishcake broth at a street vendor to thaw their cold bodies. No one cut their lips. The last one gathered all the empty cans, lids pried open. The cans made a soft clinking sound and, as if that were the cue, a bell sounded the end of lunchtime.

*

Park was in charge of the sealing process for the saury. He had always canned saury, except for the brief time he was in the mackerel line when the now-missing plant manager had just been promoted. Employees were free to switch lines as they pleased. If your stomach grew queasy at the salty, fishy smell, you could ask to be moved to the pro-

길쭉하고 날렵한 것이라면 문방구의 자도 꽁치로 보일 지경이었다. 순전히 꽁치 때문에 일을 그만둘 생각으로 그는 사장을 찾아갔다.

꽁치라면 이제 질색이에요. 차라리 고등어라면 몰라요.

고등어를 떠올린 것은 즉흥적이었다. 고등어는 공장장이 좋아하는 생선이었다. 사장이 작업복에서 풍기는 비린내에 얼굴을 찡그리며 말했다.

정 그러면 고등어 통조림도 만들어. 다른 데도 그렇게 하잖아.

그는 공장에 남았고 10년간 고등어 통조림을 만들었다. 2대 사장은 초대 사장의 장례를 치르자마자 생산 라인을 더 늘렸다. 꽁치와 고등어 통조림을 만드느라 짠내와 비린내, 기름내가 가시질 않았던 공장에 복숭아와 감귤의 향내가 당액 냄새, 구연산 냄새에 섞여 퍼지기 시작했다. 야근이 많아졌고 직원이 늘었다. 공장장이 된 그는 취임사에서 직원들에게 무엇이든 취향에 맞는 것을 선택해서 작업하라고 했다. 취향이라니. 그러니까 음악을 고르거나 영화를 고르듯이 꽁치나 고등어를, 복숭아와 감귤을 고르라는 얘기였다. 박은 고등어를 골랐

duce line and can peaches or mandarins instead. And if the lingering sweetness in the air grew dizzying, you could go back to the seafood line. That was the case in principle, but no one switched. It was the plant manager who gave workers the freedom to move around. For his first twelve years at the factory, he canned saury and only saury. Those were the factory's early days. At a certain point, anything long and slender, even a ruler at the office supply store, looked like a saury to him. He approached the president one day, wanting to quit because of the saury, and only the saury.

"I'm sick of saury now. Mackerel may be different."

Bringing up mackerel had not been planned even though he did like mackerel. The president scrunched his nose at the fish odor from the work uniform.

"If it's that bad, go and can mackerel instead. Other places let you switch, too."

He stayed at the factory and canned mackerel for the next ten years. As soon as the founding president's funeral was over, the second president expanded the production lines. The ever-present smell of salt, fish, and oil at this factory that had

다. 취향과는 상관없었다. 꽁치라면 좀 질려 있었다. 박과 마찬가지로 대개의 사람들이 꽁치를 담당했다면 고등어를, 고등어를 담당했다면 꽁치를 골랐다. 오랫동안 꽁치를 만졌던 손의 감각으로 고등어는 통통해서 잘 잡히지 않았다. 고등어를 오래 만졌던 사람들은 얇고 가느다란 꽁치를 자주 놓쳤다. 얼마 지나지 않아 꽁치든 고등어든 똑같아졌다. 품목만 달라졌을 뿐 모든 과정이 동일했다. 토막 내고 내장을 다듬고 양념하여 조리하고 밀봉한 후 살균, 냉각 과정을 거쳐 포장했다. 다시 선택한다 해도 마찬가지일 거였다. 박은 다시 담당을 바꾸었다. 생각해보니 꽁치야말로 익숙한 것을 선호하는 자신의 취향에 딱 들어맞는 생선이었다.

공장장이 갑자기 사라진 이유에 대해 여러 가지 얘기가 떠돌았다. 그중 공장장이 한 여직원과의 내연 관계가 탄로날까봐 사라졌다는 얘기가 있었다. 공장장은 술에 취하기만 하면, 그건 거의 매일이나 다름없었는데, 여직원의 집으로 찾아갔다고 했다. 여직원과 공장장이 휴일에 밖에서 만나는 걸 본 사람도 있었다. 정확한 것은 아니었다. 멀리서 본 탓이었다. 다른 여직원일 수도 있고 그저 닮은 사람일 수도 있었으며 우연히 마주친

once only canned saury and mackerel was now infused with the smell of peaches and mandarins, syrup and citric acid. Employees worked longer hours and more were hired. Upon being promoted to plant manager, he addressed the workers and told them they could choose whichever line that suited them the best. By this he meant they could choose between the saury or the mackerel, the peaches or the mandarins, just as if they were choosing between music or movies.

Park chose mackerel. It had nothing to do with how it suited him. He had simply grown tired of saury. Like Park, most people switched to mackerel from saury, or saury from mackerel. Hands that had handled saury for years had difficulty gripping the meatier mackerel. Those who had long handled the mackerel often dropped the leaner saury. Soon enough, however, handling saury and mackerel became the same. They were different products, but the process in its entirety was identical. Cut the fish into chunks, gut the innards, season, cook, seal, sterilize, cool, and package. Changing lines didn't really mean much. Park switched again. It occurred to him that preferring the familiar was what suited him best, making saury the right fish

친구의 아내일 수도 있었다. T국으로 떠나기 전이었으므로 공장장의 부인인지도 몰랐다. 소문은 삽시간에 퍼졌으나 수군거리기만 할 뿐 믿는 사람은 많지 않았다. 그는 얼굴이 검었으며 머리가 벗어지고 배가 나왔고 다리가 짧았다. 남색 작업복 양 어깨에는 비듬이 수북했고 기름 낀 머리가 목덜미 부분에서 새의 꽁지처럼 들떠 있었다. 입만 벌리면 생선 비린내나 어린아이 입냄새 같은 달큼한 냄새가 풍겼다. 한마디로 그는 연정을 품을 만한 상대가 아니었다. 소문 속 여직원은 말수가 적고 얼굴이 하얗고 좀 쌀쌀맞았다. 여직원들은 그녀가 자기들과 다르게 생겨서, 남자 직원들은 자기들을 무시하고 상대하지 않아서 불편하고 못마땅하게 생각하던 참이었다. 여직원과 공장장이 내연 관계라는 소문은 일부는 맞고 일부는 틀렸다. 집으로 찾아갔다는 소문은 맞았지만 매번 그런 것은 아니었다. 공장장의 부인이 T국으로 떠난 뒤 관계가 시작되었다는 소문도 틀린 것이었다. 여직원이 공장장을 만난 것은 그전부터였고 만나지 않게 된 것도 이미 오래전이었다. 소문 속 여직원은 공장장에 대해 한마디도 하지 않았다. 그녀가 뭔가 알고 있을 수도 있지만 그렇지 않을 수도 있었다. 여직원

for him.

Several rumors about the plant manager's sudden disappearance circulated. One was that he had had an affair with a female employee and had run away in fear of being caught. Some believed he went to her house whenever he was drunk, which was practically every night. Another claimed to have seen them out on a weekend. He was too far away to be sure, though. It could've been a different employee or a different person altogether. It could've been a coincidental run-in with a friend's wife. And still yet, it was before his wife had left for Country T, so it could've been her. Though the rumors had spread like wildfire, it was all just fodder for talk; only a few were persuaded. The plant manager had dark skin, a balding scalp, a bulging stomach, and short legs. Both shoulders of his navy blue work uniform were speckled with dandruff, and his greasy hair stuck out like a bird's tail behind his neck. His breath smelled like fish or like a kid who hadn't brushed his teeth. All this to say: there was nothing remotely attractive about him.

The rumored woman was quiet, pale-faced, and came across as cold. The female employees were uncomfortable around her because she looked dif-

의 개인적인 문제였다. 이어 횡령설이 나돌았다. 아이를 T국으로 보낸 후 줄곧 재정적인 압박을 받아왔다고 했다. 사정을 아는 사람이라면 공장에 횡령할 만한 목돈이 있을 리 없다는 것을 알았으나 누구도 적극 해명하지 않았다.

내가 귀국한다고 갑자기 남편이 나타나는 것도 아니잖아요.

전화로 총무과장에게 남편의 실종 사실을 전해 들은 공장장의 부인이 대답했다. 어학연수를 끝낸 공장장의 아이는 T국에서 상급 외국인 학교에 진학했다. 입학한 지 얼마 되지 않아 학교를 빠질 수 없었다. 학교를 빠질 수 없는 아이를 돌봐야 했으므로 공장장의 부인은 귀국할 수 없었다.

이런 경우 대부분 단순 실종이 아니라, 총무과장이 겁을 주듯 말했다. 변사 사건이라고 하던데요?

공장장의 부인이 길게 한숨을 쉬었다.

죽었더라도 마찬가지죠. 내가 간다고 살아오는 것도 아니잖아요. 만약 시체가 발견된다면 그때 가겠어요.

전화를 끊고 총무과장은 요즘 들어 자꾸 딸아이를 어학연수 보내자고 조르는 아내를 떠올렸다. 아무래도 보

ferent from them, and the men thought disapprovingly of her because she didn't associate herself with them. The suspicion that the two were having an affair was partly true. He did go to her house, but not all the time. That their relationship began after his wife left for Country T was also false. They had started seeing each other way before that, and it had already been a long time since they had stopped. The woman in the rumors did not say a word about the plant manager. She may have known something, but she may have known nothing. It was a personal matter. Then there were the embezzlement rumors. They claimed that the plant manager was under constant financial pressure because of his child in Country T. Those who knew the company's situation knew full well there was nowhere enough money to embezzle in the first place, but no one spoke out in his defense.

"It's not like my husband's suddenly going to reappear or something if I went back anyway."

The general affairs manager had called to inform the plant manager's wife about her missing husband. He'd learned that the plant manager's child had finished the course at the language institute in Country T and had been admitted into a high-

내지 않는 편이 좋을 것 같았다.

신고 후 일주일이 지나서야 조사를 시작한 형사는 공장장이 박과 사이가 좋지 않았음을 알아냈다. 실종 당일 박이 탈의실에서 공장장에게 대드는 걸 본 누군가가 형사에게 그 사실을 알렸다. 형사는 통조림 창고 안 쪽방으로 박을 불렀다. 형사가 박에게 탈의실에서 왜 공장장과 다투었는지, 공장장이 개인적인 일로 야근을 시키는 경우가 많은지, 그날 통조림을 제조하는 데 시간이 얼마나 걸렸는지, 어떤 종류의 통조림을 만들었는지, 공장에서 나와서는 무엇을 했는지, 공장장에게 여느 날과 다른 기색은 없었는지, 평소 공장장과 사이가 어땠는지를 물었고 박이 대답했다.

박의 대답이 끝나자 형사가 쪽방에서 나와 창고 쪽으로 걸어갔다. 지시는 없었으나 박은 그를 따랐다.

그날 제조한 통조림은 어떻게 했죠?

다음 날 제가 T국으로 보냈습니다, 언제나 그랬던 것처럼.

그렇게 개인적으로 통조림을 밀봉하는 일이 흔한가요?

박이 천천히 고개를 저었다. 사실 직원들 누구나 몰래

ranking international school there. And since the semester had just started, her daughter couldn't afford to miss school. And since she had to look after her daughter who couldn't afford to miss school, she couldn't come home.

"Chances are good he's not just missing," explained the general affairs manager, deliberately trying to make her worry. "I hear they're calling it a case of death by unnatural causes."

The plant manager's wife let out a long sigh.

"Even if he is dead, it doesn't change anything. He's not going to come back to life if I go back. I'll go when they find his body."

After hanging up the phone, the general affairs manager thought about his own wife and her recent plea to send their daughter to an overseas language institute. He decided against letting that happen.

The police detective, who hadn't started investigating the case until a week after the report was filed, had learned that the plant manager and Park were not on good terms. He'd been informed of this by an employee who'd heard Park confront the plant manager in the locker room on the day he was last seen. The detective called Park into a tiny

통조림에 무엇인가를 담아 밀봉해본 경험이 있었다. 공장의 누군가는 꽁치 통조림 깡통에 반지를 넣어 여자친구에게 주었다. 여자친구가 통조림 뚜껑을 열었고 은색 바닥에서 덜렁거리는 반지를 빼들었고 손가락에 끼었고 웃었다고 했다. 누군가는 아이에게 줄 크리스마스 선물로 싸구려 장난감을 통조림 깡통으로 포장했다. 원터치로 된 복숭아 통조림 뚜껑을 열면 수가 적고 단순한 레고 블록이나 비행기로만 변신하는 로봇 같은 게 나왔다. 생애 처음 장만한 집문서를 밀봉해 넣어두기도 하고 헤어진 연인에게 받은 편지를 넣어두기도 했다. 고양이를 밀봉한 직원도 있었다. 신경통으로 고생하는 부모님 때문이었다. 장터에서 고양이를 한 마리 사 와서는, 그 얘기를 들은 직원들은 분명 길을 헤매는 고양이를 주워왔을 거라고 생각했지만, 오래 끓여 국물을 우려낸 다음 헤실헤실 풀어진 고양이 살점과 함께 깡통에 담아 밀봉했다. 나중에 발각되어 시말서를 쓰기는 했지만 그 때문에 공장 사람들은 깡통에 넣어 밀봉할 수 있는 것의 종류에는 한계가 없다는 걸 새삼 깨달았다. 사장이 금고 대신 통조림 속에 현금을 넣어 보관한다는 소리도 나돌았다. 전월 회계 정산이 끝나는 월초

room inside the warehouse. He asked him about the argument in the locker room, if he was asked to work late for personal favors often, how long it took to can the foods that night, what kinds of foods were canned, what he did after leaving the factory, whether there was anything unusual about the plant manager that day, and whether they were usually on good terms.

After Park finished answering the questions, the detective walked out of the room into the warehouse. Though he wasn't asked to do so, Park followed.

"What'd you do with the cans afterwards?"

"I shipped them to Country T the next day, as usual."

"Is it common to can things like that for personal use?"

Park shook his head slowly. Truth was, all the employees had secretly canned something at least once. There was a man who sealed a ring for his girlfriend inside a saury can. When she opened the can and saw the ring lying on the can's silver bottom, she pulled it out, slid it onto her finger, and laughed in delight. There was a parent who, for Christmas once, hid some inexpensive toys in

에 사장이 직접 깡통에 지폐뭉치를 넣고 압착기를 누르고 있는 걸 누군가 봤다고 했다. 그 소문을 들은 사장이 정색하며 화를 냈다고 한 것으로 봐서는 어쩌면 사실인지도 몰랐다.

언젠가 단 둘이 남아 T국으로 보낼 통조림 만드는 일을 돕고 있을 때 공장장이 박에게 물었다.

자네는 뭘 해봤나?

네?

통조림 말이야.

박은 한 번도 통조림에 다른 것을 넣어 밀봉해본 적이 없었다. 봉인해서 간직하고 싶은 게 있을 리 없었고 밀봉한 물건을 보내줄 사람도 없었다.

실은 자네한테만 하는 말인데.

공장장이 천천히 입을 열었다.

딸아이가 유학가기 전에, 키우던 개가 죽었거든. 아이가 계속 죽은 개를 안고 울었어. 여름이어서 곧 냄새를 풍길 기세인데도 묻지 못하게 하는 거야. 안고 자는 걸 몰래 빼와서 깡통에 담아 밀봉해뒀어. 한동안 아이 방에 뒀지. 처음에는 깡통을 만지면서 울던 아이가 다른 개가 생기니까 그 깡통을 거들떠보지 않게 되더라고.

some peach cans. Pulling back the tab on the lid revealed a few Lego blocks and a robot that transformed into an airplane and other things like that.

Other canned items included documents of someone's very first home purchase and letters from a former lover. Once, someone even made canned cat meat. It was for one of her parents with neuralgia. She supposedly bought the cat from the market—people thought she found it on the street—and boiled it down for a long time until the meat became tender and loose. She canned and sealed it. She was later caught and made to write an apology but, after that incident, the factory workers realized there was no limit to what they could can. Some say that the company president stashed his cash in sealed cans instead of a safe. It was the beginning of the month after accounts were balanced when, apparently, someone saw him stuff a wad of cash inside a can and press the compressor switch. Upon hearing these rumors, the president was visibly upset—which meant it was probably true.

When Park stayed after work one day to help the plant manager can foods to send to Country T, the plant manager asked Park, "So, what did *you* do?"

"What do you mean?"

그래서 나중에는 그냥 바다에 던져 버렸어.

공장장이 검지를 입술에 가져다댔다.

비밀이야.

박이 고개를 끄덕였다. 공장장의 눈에 얼핏 말한 것을 후회하는 빛이 스쳤다. 박은 제법 입이 무겁다는 것을 증명하고 싶어 묵묵히 듣고만 있다가 침묵을 관심이 없다는 걸로 오해할까봐 입을 열었다.

개가 깡통에 들어가던가요?

작은 개였어. 가장 용량이 큰 깡통을 쓰니 딱 맞았어. 자를 필요가 없었지. 잘라야 했을 수도 있었지만, 공장장이 그 장면을 상상하듯 눈살을 찌푸렸다, 개 때문에 내 손에 피를 묻힐 수는 없잖아.

공장장이 손에 피가 묻지 않은 것을 확인하듯 손바닥을 이리저리 돌려보며 말했다.

가끔 이런 생각이 들어. 내가 죽으면 곱게 화장을 한 다음에 그 가루를 통조림 깡통 속에 보관하면 어떨까 하고 말이야. 봉분 아래서 흙과 섞여 썩어가는 것도 싫고 납골당에서 대리석 유골함에 담겨 있는 것도 싫거든. 평생 통조림 공장에서 일했고 평생 깡통만 만졌어. 깡통 재질이 변하는 거나 뚜껑 여는 방식이 달라지는

"Canning."

Park had never canned anything besides what was manufactured at the factory. He certainly had nothing valuable enough to seal, let alone someone to send a sealed item to.

"I've never told this to anyone before..."

The plant manager proceeded to speak slowly.

"Before my daughter went abroad, our dog died. She held that dead dog in her arms and wouldn't stop crying. It was summertime and the dog was bound to start smelling soon, but she wouldn't let us bury it. I had to pry it from her arms when she was finally asleep and then I canned it at the factory. We kept the can in her room for a while. In the beginning, she would stroke the can and cry, but when we got her a new dog, she didn't give the can a second glance. I ended up chucking it into the sea."

The plant manager drew his index finger to his lips.

"It's a secret."

Park nodded. The manager's eyes seemed to reveal a flash of regret that perhaps he shouldn't have told this story. Park kept silent throughout the story to indicate his future reticence, but he worried that

걸 보면서 세상이 점점 살기 편해진다는 걸 느꼈지. 깡통 포장 디자인이 바뀌는 걸 보면서 사람들 취향이 변해가는 걸 알았어. 사람들 입맛이 달라지는 건 새로 통조림이 생기거나 양념 맛이 달라지는 걸로 실감했어. 말하자면 이 깡통으로 세상을 알아간 셈이야.

세상이 깡통처럼 텅 비어 있으면 큰일인데요.

박은 곧 경솔하게 입을 놀린 걸 후회하면서도 깡통에 담겨 납골당에 가면 되겠다고 덧붙였다. 공장장이 웃음기 없는 얼굴로 박을 물끄러미 보았다. 박은 그 얼굴을 마주 보면서 공장장과 자신은 서로 다른 계절에 이동하는 철새와 같아서 절대 통할 수 없을 거라고 생각했다. 그러면서도 갑작스럽게 공장장이 그런 말을 하는 게 이상하다는 생각이 들었다. 박이 만약 무슨 일이 있는 거냐고 물어봤더라면 공장장은 자기 이야기를 더 해주었을지도 몰랐다. 그렇지만 박은 한마디도 묻지 않았다. 박이 물어보고 공장장이 대답을 했더라면 어떻게 되었을까. 물론 가정일 뿐이었다.

이렇게 큰 통조림은, 형사가 10킬로그램짜리 통조림 깡통을 손가락으로 툭툭 치면서 물었다, 주로 어디에 팝니까?

this could have been mistaken for disinterest and he mustered up a question.

"Did it fit inside the can?"

"It was a small dog. I used the largest one we had —and it was the perfect size. Didn't have to cut it. If it was just a little bigger..." He seemed to be picturing the scene. He grimaced. "Definitely don't want blood on my hands for a dog."

He inspected his hands as he spoke, as if to check for blood.

"Sometimes I think about my own death. I think I'd like to be cremated and have the ashes sealed inside a can. I don't like the idea of rotting in the soil underneath a burial mound, and I sure don't want to be stored in one of those marble urns at a crematorium. I've worked at a canning factory my whole life. My whole life I've handled cans. They're making cans with better materials now, and it's become easier to open the lids, which tells me that the world is becoming a better place to live. The changing designs of the can labels tell me that people's tastes are changing. Their actual taste for food also changes. I learn about that when new canned foods are developed or flavors are modified. In other words, I've learned about the world

수출도 하고 업소로도 나갑니다.

통조림, 좋아하시죠?

그다지 좋아하지 않아요. 오히려 싫어하는 쪽입니다.

의외라는 듯 형사가 박을 보았다.

그런데 어떻게 매일 통조림을 먹고, 10년 가까이 통조림 공장에서 일을 합니까?

저는 거의 통조림을 먹지 않아요. 맛이 없어요. 그렇다고 해서 통조림 공장에서 일하지 말란 법은 없죠. 자기가 쓰지 않는 생리대를 만드는 남자도 있는데요.

형사가 고개를 끄덕였다.

그러면 일이 재미있지는 않겠네요?

형사님도 그러시겠지만 일이라는 게 어떤 부분은 재미있지만 어떤 부분은 재미가 없지 않습니까? 저도 그래요.

그렇긴 하죠. 그런데 통조림을 만드는 건 뭐가 힘듭니까?

가끔 깡통이나 뚜껑에 손을 벱니다. 그때 기분이 상해요.

그것뿐이라면 일을 재밌어하는 쪽이군요.

비린내와 소금기를 참기 힘들죠. 기름내도 심하고요.

through this can."

"If the world were like an empty can, we'd be in trouble."

He regretted blurting this out the way he did, and added that a can of ashes could be stored at a crematorium. The plant manager looked at Park, his face void of any expression.

Looking back at his interactions with the manager, Park likened their relationship to that of two migratory birds moving in different seasons; they could never understand one another. Still, he thought it strange that the manager had disclosed something like that to him. If he had asked if everything was okay, the manager would probably have shared more. But Park hadn't asked any more. If Park had asked and the manager had answered, things could have been different. Of course, this was just an assumption.

"Big cans like this one," started the officer as he tapped on a 10-kilogram can. "Where do these mostly get sold to?"

"Some are exported, some go to businesses."

"You must like canned food."

"Not really. Actually, I dislike it."

The officer looked at Park surprised.

지금이야 밀봉을 하고 있지만 잠깐 내장을 골라내는 일을 맡았는데, 그때는 물컹거리는 건 여자 살이라도 만지기 싫었어요. 그리고 무엇보다……

깡통에 적힌 성분 표시를 읽고 있던 형사가 박에게 눈을 돌렸다.

똑같은 일이 계속 반복되지요. 저는 하루 종일 밀봉만 합니다. 어떤 사람은 하루 종일 꽁치 대가리를 치고 어떤 사람은 내내 생선 뱃속에 손가락을 넣어 미끈거리는 내장을 빼내요. 하루 종일 생선에 소금을 쳐 간을 하고, 하루 종일 깡통을 박스에 포장하기도 해요.

특별한 건 없군요. 그러면 재미있는 건 뭡니까?

박은 오래전 학교를 졸업한 후 한 번도 본 적 없는 시험지를 마주한 기분이었다. 불쾌해졌지만 자신의 대답을 건성으로 듣는 듯한 형사의 태도에 기가 눌려 성실하게 대답했다.

똑같은 일이 계속 반복되는 거예요.

형사가 장난하느냐는 눈빛으로 박을 보았다.

여기 있으면 하루 종일 벨트 위로 속을 벌린 깡통이 돌아가는 걸 봐야 해요. 어지럽죠. 빙빙 돌아요. 귀에서는 날벌레가 윙윙거리며 날아요. 자꾸 귀를 후벼파게

"How is it, then, that you can eat canned food every day and work at a canning factory for nearly ten years?"

"I barely eat the stuff. It doesn't taste good. But that's no reason not to work at a canning factory. I mean, there are men who make menstrual pads."

The officer nodded his head.

"You must not find work enjoyable then."

"I'm sure you feel the same way, officer. Don't you find some parts of work fun and others not so much? The same is true for me."

"I guess so. What's tough about making canned food?"

"Cutting your finger on the cans or the lids. It's not a good feeling."

"Other than that, everything else must not be that bad?"

"The fish odor and the saltiness are hard to bear. The smell of oil is strong, too. At least I'm in sealing now, but I used to be in the gutting line for a little bit. Back then, I didn't want to touch anything remotely tender, not even a woman's flesh. But the worst part about the job is..." The detective stopped reading the ingredient label on a can and looked up at Park.

되지요. 귀에 피딱지가 마를 날이 없어요. 어지럽고 윙윙거리고 귀가 간지러운데 매번 골똘히 궁리하는 일이라면 못 했을 거예요. 벨트 앞에 서서 그저 익숙한 각도대로 몸을 움직이기만 하면 돼요. 몸이 기계의 일부가 되어가는 거죠. 왠지 뿌듯해요. 자랑스럽지는 않지만.

형사가 건성으로 고개를 끄덕이더니 수첩을 딱 소리가 나게 덮었다. 그러고는 박에게 공장장 사택으로 안내해달라고 했다. 그는 내내 수첩을 펴들고 있었지만 아무것도 적지 않았다. 박은 여전히 형사의 기세에 눌려, 언젠가 벨트가 고장나 멈춘 줄도 모르고 이미 뚜껑을 밀봉한 깡통을 다시 뚜껑으로 밀봉한 적이 있다는 말을 삼킨 채 사택 쪽으로 걸어갔다.

독신자용 사택은 단출했다. 장기 입원 환자용으로 쓰면 딱 좋을 딱딱한 침대와 총무과에서 일괄 구입했을, 톱밥을 압축해 만든 책장과 책상, 천 소파와 서랍장이 가구의 전부였다. 조리 용기는 거의 없었다. 냉장고를 채운 것은 물과 쌀, 술과 먹다 남은 통조림을 덜어놓은 플라스틱 용기 몇 개뿐이었다. 문을 열 수 있는 수납장마다 꽁치와 고등어, 양념깻잎 통조림과 복숭아, 감귤 통조림이 들어 있었다. 싱크대 위쪽 수납장에도, 일렬

"You repeat the same things over and over. I seal cans all day long. Some people chop saury tails all day long, others take out slimy guts with their bare fingers. Some salt fish all day long, others package cans in boxes."

"Nothing special, I see. What's the fun part then?"

Park felt like he was facing an exam sheet for the first time since graduating from school. Though he was offended, the detective's halfhearted attention was overpowering, and he responded truthfully.

"The work repeats itself."

The officer's eyes seemed to ask Park if he was being serious.

"If you work here, you watch cans on conveyor belts moving around all day waiting to be filled. It's dizzying. 'Round and 'round. Winged insects buzz past your ears. You just keep sticking your finger in there. Not one day do you have a dry scab in your ear. So you're dizzy and there's buzzing and your ears itch. The job would be unbearable if you had to use your brain all day. But all you have to do is stand at the conveyor belt and move your body at the same angle and position it's grown accustomed to. You become a part of the machine. It's somewhat fulfilling. Not exactly something to be proud

로 세 개가 달린 싱크대 아래쪽 서랍에도 그랬다. 옷이 들어 있겠거니 생각하고 열어본 안방 서랍장에도 세 칸 모두 통조림뿐이었다.

이렇게 어디에나 쌓아놓고 드시는 걸 보니, 형사가 말했다. 먹을 만한가 봅니다.

박이 부엌 수납장에 있는 통조림을 종류별로 하나씩 꺼내 형사에게 건넸다.

직접 드셔보세요.

나중에 공장장님이 돌아오면 비밀로 해주셔야 합니다.

형사가 말했다.

비밀로 할 것도 없이 우리는 누구나 통조림을 먹어요. 공장에서도 먹고 집에서도 먹어요. 통조림이 월급의 일부니까요.

월급이요?

형사의 말에 박이 고개를 끄덕였다.

공장은 늘 어려우니까요. 불황은 갈수록 심각해지고요. 사장님 말로는 군소 통조림 공장이 버틸 만한 불황이 아니라고 하데요. 게다가 요새는 다들 통조림을 믿지 않아요. 유통기한이 그렇게 길다는 것 말입니다. 금

of though."

The officer nodded, clearly unimpressed, and snapped his notebook shut. Then he asked Park to take him to the plant manager's residence. The detective had kept his notebook open the entire time, but he hadn't jotted anything down. Still overpowered by the detective, Park headed towards the residence. He held his tongue about the time he accidentally sealed a lid on an already sealed can that one time the belt had unexpectedly stopped moving.

The singles housing was simple. The furniture consisted of nothing more than a stiff bed suitable for a long-term inpatient care unit, a bookcase, a desk made of compressed sawdust, a cloth-covered sofa, and a dresser. Everything but the bed had most likely been purchased in bulk by the general affairs department for all the residences. There were barely any kitchen utensils to be seen. The refrigerator contained all but some water, rice, alcohol and a few plastic containers of leftover canned food. In every drawer you could open there were cans of saury and mackerel, pickled perilla leaves, peaches and mandarins. The cabinet above the sink and the three, stacked drawers un-

방 상하지 않는 것을 불안해하죠. 산 것을 죽여서 가공한 후 죽지 않게 밀봉 처리하는 것, 그러니까 죽은 것을 상하지 않게 가공처리하여 동일한 상태를 유지하는 것. 이것이 밀봉 기술의 핵심이거든요. 모두들 그걸 수상하게 생각해요. 상하지 않으면서 동일한 상태가 지속된다는 거 말이에요. 팔리지 않으니 우리가 가져가는 겁니다. 월급의 일부로요.

통조림을 좋아하지 않는다면서 가져간 통조림은 어떻게 합니까?

저는 먹지 않지만 다른 도시에 사는 가족이나 친지들은 통조림을 먹어요. 그들에게 줍니다.

형사가 고개를 끄덕였다.

오늘 주신 통조림 말입니다, 유통기한이 얼마나 됩니까?

사택을 나와 공장 쪽으로 가려는 박에게 형사가 물었다.

제품마다 다르지만 대략 24개월에서 60개월 정도지요. 뚜껑에 인쇄되어 있어요.

길게는 5년이라…… 5년이나 상하지 않는 게 가능하다는 소리네요.

derneath the counter—cans there also. Clothes in the bedroom dresser? Alas, only cans in all three compartments.

"Seeing all these cans everywhere," noted the detective, "means they can't be that bad."

Park picked out one of each from the kitchen drawer and handed them to the officer.

"Try for yourself."

"The plant manager can't know about this if he comes back," the detective said.

"No need to keep it a secret. Anyone can have canned food if you work here. We eat it at the factory and we eat it at home. It's part of our salary."

"Your salary?"

Park nodded.

"Finances at the factory are always tight. The recession is getting worse, too. The company president said small factories like ours will have a hard time holding out. Plus, people don't trust canned food these days. It's the long shelf life that makes them have their doubts. They're wary because it doesn't go bad fast enough. Killing something and processing it so it doesn't die, in other words, processing something that's dead so it doesn't go bad and maintains its state. But, you see, that's the key

일종의 가정이지요. 유통기한 이내라면 동일한 상태가 완벽하게 유지된다고 보는 거예요. 유통기한이 지난다는 건 그런 상태가 한순간에 깨진다는 가정이고요. 그때가 되면 확인하지 않고 폐기하지요.

형사가 어깨를 으쓱해 보이고는 차에 올랐다. 그는 며칠 뒤 사장에게 전화를 걸어 공장장의 실종과 관련된 수사 상황을 알렸다. 실종에 관한 단서를 전혀 찾을 수 없기 때문에 더 이상 수사에 매진할 수 없다는 얘기였다.

to canning technology. People have suspicions about it, the fact that it lasts for such a long time without going bad, but that's just the nature of canning. Anyways, since it doesn't sell, we take it home as part of our salary."

"You said you don't like canned food. What do you with yours?"

"I don't eat it, but my family and relatives do. I give it to them."

The detective nodded.

"So when do these expire?"

He asked Park as he left the residence and headed towards the factory.

"Each product has a different shelf life, but it's anywhere from 24 to 60 months. It's printed on the lid."

"Up to five years you say... So something *can* stay good for five years."

"Well, we go by the assumption that it stays in the exact same state until the expiration date. The moment it expires, we're assuming the state is altered. That's why we don't even check expired cans before getting rid of them."

The detective shrugged nonchalantly and stepped inside his car. A few days later, he tele-

*

공장장은 없었지만 대체로 모든 일이 순조로웠다. 통조림 공장에서 일어날 법한 일들 외에 다른 일은 일어나지 않았다. 기계는 돌아갔고 통조림은 만들어졌고 기한에 맞춰 납품되었고 선적되었다. 점심시간을 알리는 종이 울리면 모두 휴게실에 모이는 것도 같았다. 뚜껑을 딴 통조림을 기준점 삼아 둥글게 모여 앉았다. 통조림 뚜껑을 딸 때는 밥을 먹는 것인지 제조 후 검사를 하는 것인지 잠시 헛갈렸으나 막상 먹기 시작하면 생산과정의 일부라는 듯 기계적으로 입을 놀렸다. 통조림을 유별나게 좋아하는 직원도 없었지만 내색하며 싫어하는 직원도 없어서 밥을 먹는 내내 모두 묵묵했다. 어느 날은 누군가 통조림에 질렸다며 탕비실에서 돼지고기를 넣은 김치찌개를 끓여왔다. 돼지고기 김치찌개라고 해서 맛이 색다르지도 뛰어나지도 않았다. 찌개를 끓이느라 허기진 시간이 길어지는 바람에 오히려 밥맛을 잃었다. 기계에서 풍기는 소음과 공장 안에 떠도는 냄새 때문에 미감을 잃어버린 게 틀림없다고 떠들어댔지만, 다음 날 시간에 쫓겨 그냥 뚜껑만 딴 통조림으로 밥을

phoned the company president and notified him of the progress of the investigation surrounding the plant manager's absence. He told him that they could no longer go through with the investigation because there were no leads.

*

Even though the plant manager had disappeared, things at the factory went pretty smoothly. Besides what you would usually expect to take place at a canning factory, there were no special occurrences. The machines did their work, the factory continued to produce canned food, cans were loaded on ships and trucks, and everything was delivered on time. When the lunch bell rang, the workers gathered in the lounges. They sat in a circle around opened cans. For a moment, as they opened the lids, they thought they were conducting a round of inspections post-manufacture. But once they started to eat, their mouths moved mechanically as if they too were a part of the production process.

No one was extremely fond of canned food, but no one expressed distaste for it either, so lunch was eaten in silence. Once, one of the employees

먹었을 때는 다시 입맛이 돌았다. 모두 통조림의 비리고 짠 맛에 익숙해져 있었다. 무감하고 무던한 식성이 고마웠다. 먹어야 할 통조림은 얼마든지 있었다.

밥을 먹은 후에는 복숭아와 감귤로 입가심을 했다. 이렇게 매일 통조림을 먹어도 될까? 누군가 물었고 점심뿐이니까 괜찮아, 하고 누군가 대답했다. 점심뿐이라면 괜찮을 테지만 그들 대부분이 점심에만 통조림을 먹는 건 아니었다. 퇴근해 집으로 돌아가서는 꽁치에 신 김치를 썰어 넣고 찌개를 끓이거나 찜을 했다. 꽁치를 다져 넣어 강된장을 만들어 고등어 통조림을 싸먹었다. 먹을거리를 사기 위해 퇴근 후 장을 보러 갔는데 자기도 모르게 공장에서 생산된 꽁치와 고등어 통조림을 장바구니에 담아버렸다고 한탄하는 직원도 있었다. 그러자 여기저기서 조용한 목소리로 자기 역시 그런 적이 있다고 고백했다. 남들은 뭐라고 해도 우리는 이걸 먹어야 하는 거 아닐까. 누군가 그렇게 말하기도 했다. 다른 회사 공장에서 만들어진 꽁치 통조림에서 구두충이 발견되었다는 뉴스가 대대적으로 보도된 날이었다. 그렇기는 하지만 순전히 의무감 때문이었다면 먹지 못했을 것이었다. 실종된 공장장의 말처럼 통조림을 먹는

made stew with *kimchi* and pork in the kitchenette and brought it back to the lounge. But she didn't find it to be particularly tasty or special. Besides, during the time it took her to make the stew, she had lost her appetite from being hungry for too long. To the others, she claimed that the noise from the machines and the various smells had ruined her taste buds. The next day, however, when limited time had her eating straight from the can with nothing but rice again for lunch, her appetite returned. They had all grown accustomed to the fishy, salty canned food. They appreciated their indifferent palates. There was more than enough food to go around.

After lunch, they cleansed their palates with peaches and mandarins. Someone asked if it was okay to have canned food so often. Another replied that once a day was fine. But for the majority of them, canned food wasn't a lunch-only ordeal. After work, they would return to their homes and put together a stew with canned saury and well-fermented *kimchi*, or braise the two together with less water. They would mash up the saury and mix it with soybean paste, which they dolloped into lettuce wraps of rice and canned mackerel.

것은 취향 탓이었다.

직원들이 통조림을 가운데 놓고 밥을 먹는 동안 박은 창고 안 쪽방에서 간단히 밥을 먹고 남는 시간에 잠을 잤다. 그 방에서는 온갖 냄새가 났다. 페놀과 아세트산 냄새, 모터에서 나는 기름 냄새, 기계에 엷게 바른 윤활유 냄새, 고무배관 냄새나 장화 냄새, 손질된 생선 내장 냄새, 벗겨진 과일 껍질 냄새가 뒤섞여 있었다. 그 냄새 탓인지 짧은 잠 속에서도 공장에서 일하는 꿈만 꿨다. 꿈속에서도 그는 벨트 앞에 서서 밀봉을 하고 있었다. 깡통에 자기 손을 넣어 밀봉했고, 빈 깡통 속에 빈 깡통 속에 빈 깡통을 넣고 밀봉하기도 했다. 어느 날의 꿈에서는 공장장이 나타나 그에게 밀봉할 것을 하나씩 건네주었다. 깡통에 넣을 수 있는 것도 넣었고 넣을 수 없는 것도 넣었다. 사장의 금고나 사장의 머리통 같은 것이었다. 공장장은 사지가 절단되어 죽어 있는 개를 주기도 했고 거대한 백골을 주기도 했다. 이걸 어떻게 넣느냐고 물으면 방앗간에서 곡식을 빻을 때 쓸 것 같은 분쇄기를 가리켰다. 박은 거침없이 분쇄기로 가서, 강도를 조절한 후 입구에 백골을 넣었다. 가루가 된 백골이 털털거리며 쏟아져 나왔다. 그 가루를 모아 깡통 속에

An employee once lamented about a time she went to buy groceries after work and caught herself putting the same cans of saury and mackerel they produced at the factory into her shopping basket. After her confession, voices began to pipe up here and there confessing that they'd done the same. Someone once asked, "Don't you think *we* should still eat this stuff regardless of what others are saying?" It was the day that news headlines reported the discovery of a spiny-headed worm inside a can of saury from another company. He had made a good point, but they wouldn't be able to eat it all the time out of obligation alone. Like the plant manager had said, eating canned food was a matter of preference.

While the others ate in the lounges, Park scarfed down his own lunch in the small room in the warehouse and slept during the time he had left. The smells inside the factory ran the gamut, from phenol and acetic acid to grease from the motors, lubricant brushed on the machines, rubber valves and rubber boots, fish guts, and fruit rinds.

Perhaps it was the smell that explained why he only dreamt about work during his short naps. In his dreams, he sealed cans as they travelled down

담았다. 백골 통조림은 외양이 같은 수천 개의 통조림에 뒤섞였다.

점심시간은 짧았다. 다시 종이 울리면 직원들은 각 구역의 휴게실에서 나와 다시 꽁치 라인 앞으로, 고등어 라인 앞으로, 깻잎 라인 앞으로, 복숭아 라인 앞으로, 감귤 라인 앞으로 걸어갔다. 쉬지 않고 흐르는 벨트 앞에서 그들은 꽁치나 고등어를 손질하고 식용 염산에 넣어 복숭아와 감귤 껍질을 벗기고. 아세트산을 넣어 가공하고, 통조림 깡통에 뚜껑이 내려와 박히는 걸 지켜보고, 임의로 통조림을 수거하여 내용물을 표본 조사했다.

작은 사고가 있기는 했다. 농산물 가공 라인에서 생긴 일이었다. 퇴근 무렵 한 여직원이 밀봉 과정에서 오른쪽 콘택트렌즈를 통조림 깡통 중 하나에 빠뜨린 게 틀림없다고 울먹였다.

어쩌다가 그랬어?

졸려서 눈을 비비다가 그런 것 같아요.

왜 이제야 알아차린 거야?

라인이 돌아가는 걸 보면 늘 어지러우니까요. 눈이 안 보이는 게 아니라 현기증이라고 생각했어요.

여직원은 일을 마치고 탈의실에서 옷을 갈아입을 때

the conveyor belt. In one particular dream, he sealed his hand inside a can. In another, he sealed an empty can inside an empty can inside an empty can. In yet another, the plant manager appeared and started to hand him objects to be sealed one after the other. Some were suitable for canning, others were not. Things like the president's safe and the president's head. He handed over a dog, dead from having its limbs amputated. When he asked how it was supposed to fit, the manager pointed to a grinder, similar to what you would see at a grain mill. Without an ounce of hesitation, Park walked to the machine, adjusted the settings, and threw the skeleton into the opening. Powdered skeleton sputtered out the other end. He collected the dustings into a can and then threw it into a pile of thousands of identical cans.

Lunchtime was short. When the bell sounded, the workers left the lounges and headed back to the saury line, the mackerel line, the perilla leaf line, the peach line, the mandarin line. They tracked cans on the conveyor belt, gutted saury and mackerel, dropped peaches and mandarins in hydrochloric acid to remove the skins, processed them in acetic acid, watched as lids were lowered

에야 눈에서 렌즈가 빠진 걸 알았다. 하루 종일 계속되던 현기증은 어지럼증이 아니라 양쪽 눈의 시력차 때문이었다. 렌즈가 붙어 있을 만한 곳을 샅샅이 뒤졌으나 찾지 못했다. 그날 하루 여직원이 담당하는 라인을 지나간 과육 통조림은 천 개가 넘었다. 갓 생산된 천 개의 통조림이 살균 과정을 마친 후 박스에 포장되기를 기다리며 줄지어 서 있었다. 벽면을 가득 채운 천 개 중 하나에 여직원이 잃어버린 콘택트렌즈가 들어 있을 것이었다. 손톱만 한 콘택트렌즈를 찾으려면 천 개의 통조림을 뜯어야 했다. 뜯어서 다시 깡통에 넣으면 그만이지만 일이 그렇게 쉬울 리 없었다. 밀봉된 통조림은 뜯는 순간 세균이 번식하기 때문에 재포장이 원칙적으로 불가능했다.

박은 난감해하는 여직원에게 말했다.

내일 아침에 콘택트렌즈를 찾았다고 말해. 작업복에 붙어 있었다고 말이야.

그러다가 나중에 무슨 일이 생기면 어쩌죠?

여직원이 걱정스럽게 물었다.

렌즈는 통조림 속에서 한 달 후에 나올 수도 있고 5년 후에 나올 수도 있고 영영 나오지 않을 수도 있어. 술집

onto cans and sealed shut, and then conducted sample inspections of cans chosen at random.

Actually, there was a *small* accident. It happened in the produce line. A female employee was on the brink of tears one late afternoon, certain that her right contact lens had fallen into a can as it was being sealed.

"What happened?"

"It must've fallen out when I was rubbing my eyes. I was sleepy."

"Why did it take so long before you realized it was gone?"

"I thought I was dizzy from watching the moving line, which is usually the case. I didn't think it was because I couldn't see."

She didn't realize her contact lens had fallen out until she was changing out of her work uniform in the locker room after work. That explained why she'd felt lightheaded all day—not from dizziness but from unbalanced vision. She searched high and low, anywhere that the lens could have fallen, but found nothing. On that day alone, more than a thousand fruit cans passed through the line she was in charge of. The thousand or so brand new fruit cans had just been sterilized and were waiting

으로 납품되면 모르고 지나가겠지. 주방장은 자기가 먹을 게 아니니까 그냥 버릴 거고, 손님들도 취해서 그냥 넘어가거나 주방의 실수로 여길 거야. 혹시 병원 같은 데로 들어가도 용케 모르고 지나갈 수도 있어. 발각될지 안 될지 모를 일을 기다리는 동안 공장 상황은 바뀔 거고 우리 상황도 바뀔지 몰라. 그렇지 않겠어?

여직원은 일단 밀봉된 통조림은 다시는 열어볼 수 없는 세계라는 걸 처음으로 이해한 듯 느릿느릿 고개를 끄덕였다.

공장장의 실종이 4개월로 접어들 무렵에 반품 사고도 있었다. 반품된 고등어 통조림은 공장장이 실종될 무렵 제조된 것이었다. 한 소비자가 슈퍼에서 구입한 고등어 통조림에서 덩어리져 뭉쳐 있는 붉은 것을 발견했다. 소비자는 고등어 피라고 생각했으나 가공 식품에 핏덩이가 있는 게 꺼림칙해 관련 기관에 신고했다. 성분 분석 결과 인혈로 밝혀져 파장이 일었다. 누군가 작업을 하다가 손을 다쳤고, 다친 손에서 흐른 피가 깡통에 새어든 것이라고 해명했다. 그 무렵 공장에서 다친 이는 아무도 없었다. 피를 흘릴 정도로 부상을 입을 만한 공정이랄 게 없었다. 설혹 손가락을 벤다고 해도 그 정도

in rows to be packaged inside boxes. Her contact lens was probably inside one of the one thousand cans that lined an entire wall. Finding the thumb-nail-sized lens would entail opening one thousand cans. It wouldn't be such a huge ordeal if the cans, once opened, could be emptied and the contents packaged in new cans. In principle, however, "re-canning" was impossible because bacteria starts to multiply the moment a sealed can is opened.

Park advised the flustered female employee.

"Tomorrow morning, tell them you found the contact lens. Say it was stuck on your uniform."

"What if it gets reported later?" she asked, much concerned.

"It could be a month or it could be five years un til that lens comes out of that can. It could also be never. A bar probably won't report it. Whoever's in the kitchen will just throw out the lens 'cause the food's not going into *their* mouth. And the custom-ers, well, they'll either be too drunk to see it or too drunk to care, anyways. Even if it ends up some-place like a hospital, it could very well go unno-ticed. In the time that we spend waiting for some-one to maybe discover it, things at the factory will change, and so may we. That makes sense, right?"

의 피를 흘렸다면 모를 리 없었다. 같은 날 제조된 통조림은 1,400개가 넘었다. 일부는 수거되었지만 대부분은 수거되지 않았다. 수거된 것 중 어떤 것에서는 인혈이 많이 발견되었고, 어떤 것에서는 거의, 어떤 것에서는 전혀 발견되지 않았다. 사장은 제조 중지 명령 기간을 단축시켜볼 요령으로 이리저리 줄을 대느라 바빴다. 누군가 인혈 얘기를 꺼낼라치면 인상부터 썼다. 과로한 사장의 눈이 인혈보다 더 붉어지고 사장의 화를 받아내느라 총무과장의 얼굴이 인혈처럼 달아올라 좀체 식지 않을 무렵, 제조 중지 명령 기간이 끝났다.

She nodded reluctantly, as if she were learning for the first time that canned food, once sealed, could never be canned again.

Approximately four months after the plant manager went missing, a can was returned to the factory. The canned mackerel had been manufactured around the same time as the manager's disappearance. A consumer had spotted a red clump in the can she had bought at the supermarket. She assumed it was fish blood, but still found it unnerving to see blood in processed food, and decided to report it. When a component analysis found the substance in question to be human blood, it caused quite the stir. The company explained that one of the employees had unknowingly cut their finger while working and that some of their blood had dripped into the can. No one had been injured around that time. No part of the work process warranted an open wound. Even if someone had cut his or her finger, there was no way it could have gone unnoticed, especially if that much blood had been spilled. The number of cans manufactured on the same day as the returned can exceeded 1,400. Some were recalled and collected, but the majority was not. Among those collected,

*

공장장의 짐은 많지 않았다. 작업복과 낡은 속옷, 몇 개의 외출복을 모두 버리고 나니 더 단출해졌다. 남은 짐은 트렁크 하나로 충분한 정도였다. 공장장의 부인은 부엌 수납장과 안방 서랍장에 있던 통조림을 모두 박에게 주었다. 기념품 삼아 몇 개 담아준 통조림도 정색하며 되돌려주었다.

어차피 아이와 나는 통조림을 먹지 않아요. 언젠가 꽁치 통조림인 줄 알고 뜯었는데……

공장장의 부인이 떠올리기 싫은 기억이라는 듯 몸서리를 쳤다.

거기서 죽은 개가 나왔어요. 그때부터 아이는 통조림이라면 질색이지요. 그러고 보니 남편이 실종되었다는 연락을 받은 며칠 후에 소포가 도착했는데 열어보니 꽁치랑 고등어 통조림이었어요. 겉은 그래도 당연히 김치나 깍두기, 그런 게 들어 있을 줄 알았는데 말이에요. 안 먹는 줄 뻔히 알면서 왜 그런 걸 보냈을까요?

공장장의 부인이 박을 바라보았다. 박은 묵묵히 부인을 마주 보았다.

some contained a great deal of blood, some barely, and some none at all. After a stop-work order was issued for the factory, the president frantically sought out his connections in an attempt to reduce the stop-work period. The president's eyes, bloodshot from fatigue, grew redder than any of the blood spots found in the cans. The face of the general affairs manager, who bore the brunt of the president's anger, flushed a bright red. Just when it seemed the collective redness of the plant would never cool, the stop-work period came to an end.

*

The plant manager didn't have much stuff. When they threw out his work uniform, some old undergarments, and the few outfits he had, not much was left. Everything fit inside a car trunk. His wife gave all the cans in the kitchen cabinets and bedroom dresser to Park. When he offered a few in return as keepsake, she sternly refused.

"My child and I don't eat canned food anymore. Imagine our surprise when I thought I was opening a can of mackerel..." The plant manager's wife shuddered at the thought, trying not to picture it

언젠가 시체라도 발견되겠죠?

공장장의 부인이 침울한 목소리로 물었다.

왜 그렇게 생각하세요. 그냥 어딘가로 잠깐 떠나 있는 걸 수도 있고……

어디로 떠날 수 있는 사람이 아닌 걸 잘 아시잖아요.

박은 대꾸할 말을 찾지 못해 입을 다물었다.

공장장의 부인이 다시 T국으로 떠난 후, 박은 공장장이 쓰던 사택으로 짐을 옮겼다. 짐이라고 해봐야 얼마 되지 않았다. 몇 장의 속옷과 가벼운 옷들이 전부여서 서랍장 두 칸이면 충분했다, 나머지 한 칸에는 가지고 있던 통조림을 넣었다. 통조림이 많지 않아 서랍장은 열고 닫을 때마다 덜렁거리는 소리를 냈다. 공장장이 남긴 통조림 중에는 유통기한이 넘은 것도 있고 임박한 것도 있고 아직 충분히 남은 것도 있었다. 시간을 들여 통조림을 종류별로 유통기한별로 깡통 크기별로 정리해서 넣어두었다.

사장은 공석이던 공장장 업무를 박에게 맡겼다. 공장장이 된 박은 직원 중 가장 먼저 출근했다. 아무도 없는 공장에서 정지한 기계의 전원을 켜는 일은 매번 낯선 개의 잠을 깨우는 것처럼 긴장되었다. 개가 짖듯 기계

again.

"There was a dead dog in there. Since then, my daughter hates anything to do with canned food. Come to think of it, a few days after I got the call about my missing husband, we got a package in the mail. There were cans of saury and mackerel inside, but I'd assumed they'd be filled with *kimchi* and *kkakdugi* as they always were. He knows we don't eat the stuff, so why'd he send it?"

She looked at Park. Park looked back.

"The body will turn up eventually, won't it?" she asked. Her tone was low and depressed.

"What are you saying? I'm sure he's just away temporarily.

"You know he's not the type to just leave like that."

Park couldn't think of a good reply and closed his mouth.

After the plant manager's wife left for Country T again, Park moved his belongings into the manager's former residence. His belongings didn't amount to much either. A few undergarments and some light clothing were all he had—two drawers of the dresser contained it all. In the remaining drawer, he stored all of the cans in his possession. There

가 요란하게 웅 소리를 내기 시작하면 그제야 하루가 시작된다는 느낌이 들었다. 퇴근은 가장 늦게 했다. 전원을 끄고 정적 속에 남아 있으면 깡통 속에 잠긴 숨죽은 꽁치나 고등어가 된 기분이었다. 꽁치나 고등어가 된 기분으로 사택에 돌아가 몸을 절이듯 술을 마셨다. 잠을 푹 자기 위해서였다. 가장 먼저 출근하고 가장 늦게 퇴근하는 그를 직원들이 수위라고 놀리는 걸 알고 있었지만 모른 척했다. 일찍 출근하게 되면서 공복 시간이 길어지고 숙취로 속이 쓰리기도 해서 아침밥을 먹기로 했다. 망설이다가 서랍장에 넣어둔 통조림을 꺼내 뜯었다. 뼈와 살을 함께 얼마쯤 천천히 씹고 나자 꽁치에 스며 있던 양념이 입 안에 퍼졌다. 짜고 비릿한 느낌이 차츰 사라졌다. 처음에는 생각보다 맛이 괜찮은 정도였다. 좀더 먹자 고소한 맛이 풍기는 것 같았다. 점심시간에는 직원들과 어울려 뚜껑을 딴 통조림으로 밥을 먹었다.

어? 공장장님 원래 통조림 안 드셨잖아요.

함께 점심을 먹기 시작하고 한참이 지난 후에 누군가 박이 꽁치 토막을 입에 떠넣는 걸 보고 물었다. 박은 꽁치 국물이 스민 흰 밥을 입에 넣으며 씩 웃었다. 밥을 먹

weren't many, so the drawer rattled whenever it opened or closed. Among the cans the plant manager left behind, some had expired, some were close, and some were far from it. Park took the time to organize them by type, expiration date, and size.

The company president appointed Park to take over the duties of plant manager. As the new plant manager, Park had to show up at the factory before everyone else. Flipping the power switches to the machines that had been turned off for the night was like waking an unfamiliar dog from its slumber; it made him nervous each morning. As a woken dog will bark, so the machines also began to make low rumbles and roars when first activated. For Park, the day didn't begin until he heard that sound. He was the last to go home as well. He stood in the silence after the machines were powered down. He had become one of the saury or mackerel in the cans, lifeless and locked in.

And like fish is preserved in brine, he drank when he returned to the residence. He drank so he could sleep soundly. He knew the employees secretly referred to him as Security Guard for being the first in and last out, but he pretended not to know. Be-

은 후에는 직원들과 함께 복숭아와 감귤 통조림을 먹었다. 양치를 해도 입 안에 달짝지근한 맛이 남았다. 하루 종일 사탕을 물고 있는 기분이었다. 나쁘지 않았다. 퇴근 후에는 사택에 돌아가 통조림 중 하나를 꺼내 김치를 넣고 요리를 하거나 다져서 양념장을 만든 후에 술안주로 먹었다.

서랍장에 넣어둔 것을 다 먹어, 처음으로 전(前) 공장장의 통조림을 땄을 때 박은 당황해서 깡통 포장과 내용물을 번갈아 보았다. 몇 개인가 통조림 뚜껑을 더 따 보고 나서는 웃음을 터뜨렸다. 통조림은 한마디로 엉망진창이었다. 포장과 내용물이 뒤죽박죽이었다. 꽁치 통조림을 따면 꽁치가 나오기도 했지만 고등어나 양념깻잎이 나왔다. 고등어 통조림을 따면 고등어가 나올 때도 있었지만 깻잎이나 꽁치가 나왔다. 과일 통조림도 마찬가지였다. 어떤 통조림은 T국으로 보내려고 했던 것인 듯 콩장이나 멸치볶음 같은 게 나왔고 오래되어 곰팡이가 피고 쉰내를 풍기는 물컹해진 감자조림도 나왔다. 무엇이든 뚜껑을 열어보기 전까지는 내용물을 알 수 없었다. 박은 꽁치 통조림에 들어 있는 고등어를, 고등어 통조림에 든 콩장을, 깻잎 통조림에 든 깻잎을 먹

ing at work so early, he was hungrier longer, and the alcohol from the night before didn't help either. So he decided to have breakfast before heading out. After hesitating about it a little, he opened one of the cans in his drawer. At first, he found that it tasted better than he'd expected. The more he had of it, it even began to taste rich. At lunchtime, he sat with the employees around opened cans and ate as they did.

"Wait, you didn't eat canned food before."

A long time after Park started joining them for lunch, one of the workers remarked on this after watching Park put a chunk of saury in his mouth. Park followed it with a spoonful of white rice smeared with saury juice, and grinned. After the meal, Park would have canned peaches and mandarins with the others. Brushing his teeth didn't get rid of the sugary taste in his mouth. It was like sucking on candy all day long. It wasn't bad. After work, he would prepare a dish using some *kimchi* and one of the canned food items at home to accompany the alcohol. Either that or he would crush the canned fish and mix it with soybean and red pepper paste.

When the drawer was empty, he turned to the

으며 자신이 처음으로 공장장 때문에 웃었다는 생각을 했다.

통조림에서 먹을 것만 나오는 것은 아니었다. 빨지 않은 채로 밀봉되어 역한 냄새를 풍기는 양말과 속옷 뭉치가 나오기도 했다. T국으로 송금한 내역서가 여러 장 나왔고 T국의 딸아이에게서 받은 영어 편지가 서너 통 나왔다. 여러 달치 급여명세서와 연금을 받으려고 붓고 있던 적금 내역과 생명보험 약정서가 나왔다. 공장장의 이름이 이니셜로 새겨진 열쇠고리가 또 다른 이니셜이 새겨진 열쇠고리와 함께 나왔다. 신용카드 영수증이 나왔을 때는 꼼꼼히 내역을 살펴보았다. 오래전 누군가와 만나 밥을 먹고 차를 마시고 영화를 본 내역이 고스란히 남아 있었다. 뭔가 나올 때마다 유심히 보기는 했지만 마음이 편치 않았다. 뜻하지 않게 공장장의 삶에 끼어든 것 같아서였다.

통조림 뚜껑을 딸 때면 겁이 나기도 했다. 여전히 깡통 안에서는 뭐가 나올지 알 수 없었다. 어느 날인가 피 냄새에 섞여 곯은 내를 풍기는 정체 모를 뼈와 살덩어리 같은 게 나온다면, 어쨌거나 공장장은 죽은 개를 밀봉한 적도 있는 사람이었으므로, 박은 고심하다가 그것

cans left behind by the previous manager. When he opened one, he was confused and double-checked the label. He opened several more and broke out into laughter. The can labels and contents were all jumbled up. Some of the saury cans contained saury, but some contained mackerel or pickled perilla leaves. Some of the mackerel cans contained mackerel, but some contained perilla leaves or saury. The fruit cans were all mixed up as well. Some of them contained stewed beans or stir-fried anchovies. One of them had moldy braised potatoes. They were so old they had broken down and smelled sharp and sour. You had no idea what was inside until you opened the can. As Park ate the mackerel from the saury can, the beans from the mackerel can, and the perilla leaves from the perilla leaves can, he realized that this was the first time he had laughed because of something the plant manager had done.

There weren't just food items stored in the former manager's cans. Park found a bundle of dirty socks and underwear in one, the socks foul and pungent. In another, he found a receipt for a wire transfer to Country T. Three or four of them contained letters written in English from the manager's

을 들고 공장으로 가기로 했다. 용량이 큰 깡통을 가져다가 손에 피가 묻지 않게 조심하면서 내용물을 옮겨 담은 후에 압착기로 뚜껑을 내리누를 거였다. 피식 소리가 나면서 깡통 안에 고여 있던 공기가 빠져 나가면 썩어 냄새를 풍기던 뼈와 살덩어리는 다시 얼마간 비밀을 품은 채 깡통 속에 고요히 밀봉될 거였다. 그것은 박이 꽁치나 고등어 이외의 것을 넣어 밀봉한 첫 번째 통조림이 될 거였다. 박은 이제 막 천천히 칼날을 움직여 뚜껑을 딴 통조림의 내용물을 오랫동안 들여다보며 생각했다. 전 공장장도 아마 그렇게 했을 거라고.

『저녁의 구애』, 문학과지성사, 2011

daughter in Country T. Several months' worth of paystubs from work, a bank statement for an installment savings account he opened as part of a pension plan, and a signed life insurance policy.

There were two key chains with a set of initials engraved on each—the manager's and someone else's. Park found credit card receipts in yet another, which he inspected carefully. They were quite dated. The plant manager had met with someone for a meal, a cup of coffee, and a movie afterwards. Park looked closely at what he came across, but it didn't feel right. He didn't mean to intrude in the plant manager's life.

He was slightly afraid of opening the cans now. There was no telling what was inside of them. Park thought long and hard about what he would do if, say, he discovered a can of unidentifiable flesh and bones smelling of spoiled food and blood. After all, the plant manager had even canned a dead dog before. He decided he would take the opened can back to the factory. He would be careful not to get any blood on his hands, move the contents into one of the larger cans, and use the compressor to seal it shut. It would make a tight, hissing sound as the air inside escaped. Then, the decaying, reeking bundle of flesh and bones would be sealed shut inside a can again, its secret safe for another period of time. That would be the first time Park ever sealed something inside a can other than saury or mackerel. Park looked long and hard at the contents of the can. He reasoned that the former plant manager would have done the same.

Translated by Michelle Jooeun Kim

해설

Afterword

통조림으로 압축한 근대체제론

전철희 (문학평론가)

「통조림 공장」은 어느 날 불현듯 실종된 공장장의 이야기로 시작된다. 일반적인 소설의 문법을 따른다면 이런 서두 뒤에는 으레 공장장이 사라진 이유가 무엇인지, 사라진 그는 어떻게 되었는지, 실종사건 이후 공장에서는 어떤 사건이 벌어졌는지 등에 관한 설명이 이어져야 한다. 그러나 「통조림 공장」은 이 의문 중 어느 하나에 대해서도 제대로 답하지 않는다. 작가가 불성실해서 그런 것은 아니다. 공장장을 비롯한 인물들이 아니라, 통조림 공장과 그 공장에서 만드는 통조림에 작품의 초점이 맞춰져 있기 때문이다.

그런 연고로 이 작품을 살펴보기 위해서는 먼저 통조

Modern Systems Theory Compressed in a Can

Jeon Cheol-hee (literary critic)

"The Canning Factory" by Pyun Hye-young begins with a story of a factory manager who suddenly goes missing. Any reader would require an explanation as to why this happened, what happened to him, and what happened to the factory afterwards. "The Canning Factory," however, does not properly address any of these questions, instead focusing on the factory itself, the canned food, and a host of other characters.

To study Pyun's story from this frame of mind requires a review of the properties of canned food. The innovation of canned food has made food preservation far easier, extending the shelf life of fruits, vegetables, and meats exponentially. The

림의 성질을 고찰해야 한다. 통조림은 보관과 조리의 수고를 대거 감소시켜준 혁신적 발명품이다. 그것은 과일이나 채소, 고기 등의 유통기간을 기하급수적으로 늘여주었다. 더욱이 그 속의 식재료는 대개 기본적인 가공과 손질을 마친 상태이기 때문에 먹는 사람이 손질이나 요리를 할 수고도 제거해준다. 하지만 편혜영은 편리함의 이면에 똬리를 튼 야만성을 주시한다. 통조림 속에는 엄청난 방부제가 있다. 방부제는 통조림의 내용물이 신선하지는 않을지언정 썩지는 않은 상태로 만든다. 그로 말미암아 통조림의 내용물은 유기물도 무기물도 아닌 무언가가 된다. 과학문명으로 생명의 여하까지 통제할 수 있게 되었다는 사실이 왠지 찝찝하게 느껴지는 대목이다.

그러나 더 큰 문제는 통조림을 대량생산하기 위해 동원된 공장의 노동자들 역시 같은 입장이라는 점이다. 그들은 매일 같은 시간 같은 공간에서 같은 일을 한다. 노동과정에 개인의 창의성 따위가 개진될 여지는 없다. 오직 생계를 영위하기 위해 그들은 단순노동에 숙달돼야 하고, 그 과정에서 삶도 획일화되어간다. 반복노동의 일부를 맡은 그들의 삶은 하등 기계와 구별되지 않

ready-to-eat food inside the cans translates to less work in the kitchen and, yet, behind this convenience lies an unleashed savagery. The process of canning utilizes an incredible amount of preservatives, keeping the food from rotting—not staying fresh. The contents of canned goods are, then, neither organic nor inorganic, but somewhere in between. The fact that our civilization can use science to control the lifespan of living things can be a bit unsettling.

The greater issue here, though, is that the people working in these factories are often not much different. The daily, monotonous routines of the unnamed workers in "The Canning Factory" do not allow for any self-expression in the work process. They need to be proficient in simple tasks to sustain their lives while everything about them becomes uniform along the way. As they play their part in the repetitive labor of mass production, they become no different from the inferior machines they run. Pyun likens the laborers in her story to the food sealed inside the cans, neither living nor dead, but somewhere in the middle.

The process of canning adds life to dead ingredients and takes the life out of those doing the

는다. 유기물도 무기물도 아닌 어정쩡한 존재라는 점에서 통조림 속에 밀봉된 식료품과도 다를 바 없는 처지라고 하겠다.

요컨대 통조림은 죽어 있는 식재료에 신선도를 부여하고, 또한 살아 있는 노동자를 죽어 있는 존재처럼 만든다. 생명 여하까지를 관장하는 통조림과 공장은 현대의 사회구성체를 상징한다. 통조림은 보관 기술의 혁신과 식생활에서까지 합리성을 추구하는 근대문화의 반영이자 산업화 이후 불붙은 핵가족화(가족붕괴)의 부산물이다. 노동자 역시 공업혁명의 결과임은 부연할 필요도 없다. 소설 속 통조림에는 유기된 고양이, 집에서 기르던 개, 어쩌면 사람의 시체까지를 포함한 모든 것을 담을 수 있다. 어떤 것도 한 번 담기고 나면 똑같은 규격의 통조림 모양이 된다. 공장 역시 모든 사람을 획일적 형질로 바꿔놓는다. 가장 극적인 예는 소설 속에서 '수위'라는 별명으로 불리는 공장장이다. 그는 다소 비윤리적인 도덕관념이 몸에 배어 있을지언정, 성실한 회사원으로서 하위 직원을 관리하는 일에 충실했다. 그 충실성은 노동자들에게 그가 어떤 성찰도 없이 무미건조하게 공장 배회를 반복할 뿐인, 그래서 인간적인 유대감

work. The canned food and the canning factory here symbolize the components of modern society. Canned food reflects the pursuit of rationality in modern culture, extending to innovative preservation technologies and even dining habits. At the same time, it is a byproduct of multigenerational family collapse sparked by the heavy industrialization we see in our society today. The laborer, too, is an undeniable result of industrial revolution. The contents of the cans in the story range from everything to an abandoned cat, a pet dog, and possibly even a human body. Whatever it may have been beforehand, the contents of the cans in Pyun's story end up in the same-sized can afterwards.

The factory, too, turns its workers into uniform beings. The most extreme example of this is the plant manager, nicknamed "Security Guard" by the employees. Though he exhibits a slightly unethical sense of morals, he is diligent taskmaster and manager. It is because of this diligence that the other employees see him as a security guard, wandering about the factory without any introspection and thus unable to form any personal ties with others. After he goes missing, Park takes on the position of plant manager. Interestingly enough, he also inher-

을 맺을 여지 따위는 없는 '수위'로 보이게 만들었다. 그가 사라지고 박이 공장장직을 인계받는다. 흥미로운 것은 이때 그가 '수위'라는 별명까지 물려받게 된다는 사실이다. 다른 누가 공장장이 되어도 상황은 크게 다르지 않았을 것이다. 전임 공장장의 비인간적인 모습은 그의 개인적인 문제가 아니라 공장장이라는 직위가 만든 것이었기 때문이다. 공장이란 체제는 모든 인간의 개별성을 소거시켜 특정 직위에 걸맞은 사람으로 만들어버리는 익명의 공간이다. 마치 어떤 재료도 규격화시켜버리는 통조림이 그렇듯 말이다.

물론 근대 사회가 여러모로 이전 체계보다 진보했음은 의심할 바 없다. 문제는 그런 사회의 진보가 동시에 인간성을 말살할 때도 있다는 점이다. 편혜영의 소설은 통조림과 공장을 통해 근대화가 지닌 파멸적 속성을 묘사한다. 구체적인 대상을 통해 육화되는 까닭에 무기적 존재가 되는 현대인의 초상은 생생하게 표현된다. 그녀의 소설은 어떤 자극적인 장면도 제시하지 않고 서사의 전개 방향을 바꿀 만한 반전이나 사건 따위를 지니지도 않은 채, 담담한 묘사만으로 이 변화 없는 세상의 공포를 담아냈다.

its the nickname "Security Guard." No matter the replacement, Park clearly seems to be suggesting the nicknaming results would have been the same. It is the position of plant manager that makes its officer seem inhumane; it has nothing to do with his personality. The factory system eliminates all individuality and makes everyone fit a certain position—like the ingredients packed into a can.

It goes without saying that modern society has advanced in many regards, but these advances have also destroyed a certain degree of humanity at the same time. Pyun Hye-young's story employs canned food and canning factories to depict the destructive nature of modernization. It draws a vivid portrait of contemporary man as a sort of dead being. There are no provocative scenes or surprise twists in the plot. The flat, almost indifferent narration aptly captures a fear of this unchanging world.

Even before the release of "The Canning Factory," Pyun Hye-young has delved into the task of story-telling the irrationalities and estrangements created by modern society. She expressed her awareness of problems in various ways depending on her work. Her earlier stories, for example, demonstrated how traumatic circumstances threw

「통조림 공장」을 발표하기 전부터 편혜영은 현대 사회가 빚어낸 부조리와 소외의 양태를 소설화시키는 작업에 천착해왔다. 그녀의 문제의식은 작품에 따라 다양한 방법으로 구현되곤 했다. 그녀의 초창기 소설은 외상적(traumatic) 사건에 마주한 인물들이 파국에 다다르는 과정을 담아냈다. 그 속에서 현실은 그로테스크하고 섬뜩(gore)한 이미지를 통해 표현됐다. 소설집의 출간이 거듭될수록 편혜영은 소설에서 자극적 이미지를 제거하고, 근대체제의 병폐를 구체적인 현실로 모사하는 작업에 나아갔다. 「통조림 공장」은 작가의 세 번째 소설집 『저녁의 구애』에 수록된 작품으로, 그녀의 변화가 어느 정도 진행된 상황에서 쓰였다. 세련된 알레고리와 명확한 문제의식이 돋보이는 그녀의 작품은 문학의 사소설적 성격과 현실참여적 속성이 강조되던 한국의 문단에서 특출한 개성이자 오롯한 성취로 평가받고 있다.

people into catastrophe. Here, though, the realities of labor are expressed through grotesque, gory imagery. Pyun's works have grown cooly objective over time as she has copied the ills of the modern system onto concrete realities. "The Canning Factory" is part of her third collection entitled *Evening Courtship,* and was written after this change had started to take place. Marked by refined allegory and definite problem-awareness, Pyun Hye-young's works are complete literary achievements, brimming with an exceptional individuality in any South Korean literary circle, which often merely feature works that are autobiographical and fused with only certain notions of reality.

비평의 목소리

Critical Acclaim

편혜영은 우리가 살고 있는 세계를 둘러싸고 있는 화려한 피막(皮膜)을 걷어내고, 그 아래 존재하는 공포스러운 디스토피아를 보여준 바 있다. 그녀의 세계에서 수성(獸性)과 질병은 우리가 살고 있는 세계의 안전성을 의심하게 만들면서 안개 같은 몽롱한 손길로 우리의 목을 졸랐다.

허윤진

그녀에게 문학은 (과거가 아니라) 현재를 향하는 것이고, (바깥에서 안을 지향하는 것이 아니라) 안에서 바깥을 지향하는 것이며, (80년대적인 것이나 90년대적인 것과는 다르

Pyun Hye-young lifts away the flashy membrane that encloses our world to reveal the frightening dystopia underneath. The savagery and ills in her world silently choke us and lead us to question the safety of the world in which we live.

Heo Yun-jin

Literature to her points to the present (and not the past), looks out (and not in), and is about the new millennium (different from the 80s or 90s). To write a new story that cuts this era open and rips out its guts—this is the author's ambition. And when ambition meets talent, history is made. Shin Hyeong-cheol

다는 뜻에서) 2000년대적인 어떤 것이다. 지금 이 시대의 배를 갈라 그 내장을 섬뜩하게 꺼내드는 새로운 소설을 쓰겠다는 것, 이것이 이 작가의 욕망이다. 욕망이 재능을 만나면 역사가 된다.

신형철

인간의 사소한 감정들을 무턱대고 분출하지 않으면서도 일상의 작은 기미들을 포착하는 정확한 능력에 있어서라면, 그리고 그 사소한 기미들이 세계의 거대한 비밀을 건드리는 데까지 나아가도록 이끄는 과감한 솜씨에 대해서라면 편혜영은 시작부터 고수였다.

조연정

이제 편혜영의 소설은 더 이상 하드고어적 상상력에 기대고 있지는 않은 듯하다. 그런데 나는 『저녁의 구애』의 편혜영이 더 섬뜩하고 무섭다. 억압된 야만의 귀환이나, 자연의 복수보다 더 공포스러운 것은, 우리가 안온하다고, 편안하다고 느끼는 이 문명 자체가 이미 어떠한 차이도 용인되지 않는 야만적인 자연이자 동일성의 지옥이라는 그 사실이다.

김형중

In terms of effortlessly capturing the smallest indications of everyday life without triggering intricate human emotions... In terms of taking those intricacies and probing into the world's great secrets... Pyun Hye-young has been a master from the start.

Cho Yeon-jeong

Pyun Hye-young's stories no longer seem to lean on a gory imagination, but I find the Pyun Hye-young of *Evening Courtship* to be more eerie and frightening. More horrifying than the return of suppressed barbarism or the vengeance of nature, is the fact that the civilization we think to be safe and secure is, in fact, a barbaric place that has no tolerance for differences, a hell of uniformity.

Kim Hyeong-jung

편혜영

1972년 서울에서 태어나 서울예술대학교 문예창작학과와 한양대학교 국어국문학과 대학원을 졸업했다. 현재 명지대학교 문예창작학과 교수로 재직 중이다. 2000년 서울신문 신춘문예에 단편「이슬털기」가 당선되며 작품 활동을 시작했다. 2005년 그로테스크한 이미지를 통해 화려한 문명사회의 어두운 배면을 폭로한 첫 소설집『아오이 가든』을 출간하며 문단의 주목을 받았다. 평론가 이광호는 이 소설집이 "문명의 미끈함과 자연스러움을 충격적으로 벗겨낸다"면서 "한국 소설의 특별한 '또 다른 시작'"이라고 평가했다. 2007년 두 번째 소설집『사육장 쪽으로』를 출간했다. 절제된 문체로 현대인의 소외와 불안을 디테일하게 묘사했다는 점을 인정받아 한국일보문학상을 받았다. 2009년 단편소설「토끼의 묘」를 통해 이효석문학상을 수상했다. 2010년 첫 장편소설『재와 빨강』을 상재하고 오늘의 젊은 예술가상을 받았다.『재와 빨강』은 카프카의 소설에서처럼 억울한 상황에 처한 인물을 등장시켜 현대인의 인간성 상실과

Pyun Hye-young

Pyun Hye-young was born in Seoul in 1972. She majored in creative writing at Seoul Institute of the Arts and earned a graduate degree in Korean literature at Hanyang University. She is currently a professor of creative writing at Myongji University. She made her literary debut in 2000 when her short story, "Shaking off the Dew," won the Spring Literary Contest hosted by *the Seoul Shinmun*. She started drawing attention from literary circles after her first collection of stories was published in 2005. *Aoi Gardens* exposed the dark interior of an ostentatious civilized society through grotesque imagery. Critic Lee Kwang-ho remarked that the collection "peels off the sleek and natural-looking skin of civilization in an appalling manner," and "marks a new beginning of Korean novels."

Her second collection *To the Kennels* was published in 2007. It received *the Hankook Ilbo* Literary Award for depicting in great detail and restrained voice the alienation and anxiety of the modern individual. In 2009, her short story "The Rabbit's

고독을 묘파한 작품이었다. 2011년 단편집『저녁의 구애』를 발간했다. 예외성 없이 반복되는 현대인의 일상을 섬뜩하게 묘사했다는 점을 인정받아 동인문학상을 수상했다. 2012년 장편『서쪽 숲에 갔다』를, 2013년 단편집『밤이 지나간다』를 각각 출간했다. 편혜영의 작품은 절제되고 단단한 문체를 기반으로 삼아 현대인의 불안을 묘사하고, 그 불안을 야기한 근대 사회 체제의 소외와 고독을 비판한다. 창작 활동을 이어가는 동안 꾸준히 자기 갱신을 거듭하면서도 자신만의 독창적인 작품세계를 구축했다고 평가받는다. 2000년대 한국문학을 대표하는 작가 중 한 명으로 여전히 많은 독자와 평론가들의 이목을 집중시키고 있다.

Grave" won the Yi Hyo-seok Literary Award. She was commended as "Today's Young Artist" when her first full-length novel, *Ashes and Red,* was published in 2010. Similar to works by Franz Kafka, *Ashes and Red* features characters in helpless situations, depicting the dehumanization and isolation of modern society. *Evening Courtship,* published in 2011, received the Dongin Literary Award for its ghastly portrayal of the routine life of the contemporary man. Her novel *I Went to the Forest in the West* was published in 2012, followed by her story collection *The Night Passes* the next year.

In her restrained, yet grounded writing style, Pyun Hye-young's works portray the insecurities of contemporary man and point to the contemporary system for causing this sense of alienation and isolation. She is noted for renewing herself piece by piece and building her own unique world of writing in the process. As already one of the great representative writers of Korean literature in the 2000s, she continues to draw the interest of many readers and critics.

번역 **미셸 주은 김** Translated by Michelle Jooeun Kim

미셸 주은 김(김주은)은 버지니아 주립대학교 국제학과를 졸업하고 한동대학교 통역번역대학원에서 석사학위를 받았다. 이승우 단편소설 「칼」의 번역으로 한국문학번역원 제11회 한국문학번역신인상을 수상하였다.

Michelle Jooeun Kim studied Foreign Affairs at the University of Virginia and received her master's degree in Applied Linguistics and Translation at Handong University's Graduate School of Interpretation and Translation. She received the 11th Korean Literature Translation Award for New Translators with Lee Seung-u's short story "The Knife."

감수 **전승희, 데이비드 윌리엄 홍**

Edited by Jeon Seung-hee and David William Hong

전승희는 서울대학교와 하버드대학교에서 영문학과 비교문학으로 박사 학위를 받았으며, 현재 하버드대학교 한국학 연구소의 연구원으로 재직하며 아시아 문예 계간지 《ASIA》 편집위원으로 활동 중이다. 현대 한국문학 및 세계문학을 다룬 논문을 다수 발표했으며, 바흐친의 『장편소설과 민중언어』, 제인 오스틴의 『오만과 편견』 등을 공역했다. 1988년 한국여성연구소의 창립과 《여성과 사회》의 창간에 참여했고, 2002년부터 보스턴 지역 피학대 여성을 위한 단체인 '트랜지션하우스' 운영에 참여해 왔다. 2006년 하버드대학교 한국학 연구소에서 '한국 현대사와 기억'을 주제로 한 워크숍을 주관했다.

Jeon Seung-hee is a member of the Editorial Board of ***ASIA***, and a Fellow at the Korea Institute, Harvard University. She received a Ph.D. in English Literature from Seoul National University and a Ph.D. in Comparative Literature from Harvard University. She has presented and published numerous papers on modern Korean and world literature. She is also a co-translator of Mikhail Bakhtin's ***Novel and the People's Culture*** and Jane Austen's ***Pride and Prejudice***. She is a founding member of the Korean Women's Studies Institute and of the biannual Women's Studies' journal ***Women and Society*** (1988), and she has been working at 'Transition House,' the first and oldest shelter for battered women in New England. She organized a workshop entitled "The Politics of Memory in Modern Korea" at the Korea Institute, Harvard University, in 2006. She also served as an advising committee member for the Asia-Africa Literature Festival in 2007 and for the POSCO Asian Literature Forum in 2008.

데이비드 윌리엄 홍은 미국 일리노이주 시카고에서 태어났다. 일리노이대학교에서 영문학을, 뉴욕대학교에서 영어교육을 공부했다. 지난 2년간 서울에 거주하면서 처음으로 한국인과 아시아계 미국인 문학에 깊이 몰두할 기회를 가졌다. 현재 뉴욕에서 거주하며 강의와 저술 활동을 한다.

David William Hong was born in 1986 in Chicago, Illinois. He studied English Literature at the University of Illinois and English Education at New York University. For the past two years, he lived in Seoul, South Korea, where he was able to immerse himself in Korean and Asian-American literature for the first time. Currently, he lives in New York City, teaching and writing.

바이링궐 에디션 한국 대표 소설 068
통조림 공장

2014년 6월 6일 초판 1쇄 인쇄 | 2014년 6월 13일 초판 1쇄 발행

지은이 편혜영 | **옮긴이** 미셸 주은 김 | **펴낸이** 김재범
감수 전승희, 데이비드 윌리엄 홍 | **기획** 정은경, 전성태, 이경재
편집 정수인, 이은혜 | **관리** 박신영 | **디자인** 이춘희
펴낸곳 (주)아시아 | **출판등록** 2006년 1월 27일 제406-2006-000004호
주소 서울특별시 동작구 서달로 161-1(흑석동 100-16)
전화 02.821.5055 | **팩스** 02.821.5057 | **홈페이지** www.bookasia.org
ISBN 979-11-5662-018-1 (set) | 979-11-5662-030-3 (04810)
값은 뒤표지에 있습니다.

Bi-lingual Edition Modern Korean Literature 068
The Canning Factory

Written by Pyun Hye-young I **Translated by** Michelle Jooeun Kim
Published by Asia Publishers I 161-1, Seodal-ro, Dongjak-gu, Seoul, Korea
Homepage Address www.bookasia.org I **Tel**. (822).821.5055 I **Fax**. (822).821.5057
First published in Korea by Asia Publishers 2014
ISBN 979-11-5662-018-1 (set) | 979-11-5662-030-3 (04810)

〈바이링궐 에디션 한국 대표 소설〉 작품 목록(1~60)

아시아는 지난 반세기 동안 한국에서 나온 가장 중요하고 첨예한 문제의식을 가진 작가들의 작품들을 선별하여 총 105권의 시리즈를 기획하였다. 하버드 한국학 연구원 및 세계 각국의 우수한 번역진들이 참여하여 외국인들이 읽어도 어색함이 느껴지지 않는 손색없는 번역으로 인정받았다. 이 시리즈는 세계인들에게 문학 한류의 지속적인 힘과 가능성을 입증하는 전집이 될 것이다.

바이링궐 에디션 한국 대표 소설 set 1

분단 Division

01 병신과 머저리-**이청준** The Wounded-**Yi Cheong-jun**

02 어둠의 혼-**김원일** Soul of Darkness-**Kim Won-il**

03 순이삼촌-**현기영** Sun-i Samch'on-**Hyun Ki-young**

04 엄마의 말뚝 1-**박완서** Mother's Stake I-**Park Wan-suh**

05 유형의 땅-**조정래** The Land of the Banished-**Jo Jung-rae**

산업화 Industrialization

06 무진기행-**김승옥** Record of a Journey to Mujin-**Kim Seung-ok**

07 삼포 가는 길-**황석영** The Road to Sampo-**Hwang Sok-yong**

08 아홉 켤레의 구두로 남은 사내-**윤흥길** The Man Who Was Left as Nine Pairs of Shoes-**Yun Heung-gil**

09 돌아온 우리의 친구-**신상웅** Our Friend's Homecoming-**Shin Sang-ung**

10 원미동 시인-**양귀자** The Poet of Wŏnmi-dong-**Yang Kwi-ja**

여성 Women

11 중국인 거리-**오정희** Chinatown-**Oh Jung-hee**

12 풍금이 있던 자리-**신경숙** The Place Where the Harmonium Was-**Shin Kyung-sook**

13 하나코는 없다-**최윤** The Last of Hanak'o-**Ch'oe Yun**

14 인간에 대한 예의-**공지영** Human Decency-**Gong Ji-young**

15 빈처-**은희경** Poor Man's Wife-**Eun Hee-kyung**

바이링궐 에디션 한국 대표 소설 set 2

자유 Liberty

16 필론의 돼지-**이문열** Pilon's Pig-**Yi Mun-yol**

17 슬로우 불릿-**이대환** Slow Bullet-**Lee Dae-hwan**

18 직선과 독가스-**임철우** Straight Lines and Poison Gas-**Lim Chul-woo**

19 깃발-**홍희담** The Flag-**Hong Hee-dam**

20 새벽 출정-**방현석** Off to Battle at Dawn-**Bang Hyeon-seok**

사랑과 연애 Love and Love Affairs

21 별을 사랑하는 마음으로-**윤후명** With the Love for the Stars-**Yun Hu-myong**
22 목련공원-**이승우** Magnolia Park-**Lee Seung-u**
23 칼에 찔린 자국-**김인숙** Stab-**Kim In-suk**
24 회복하는 인간-**한강** Convalescence-**Han Kang**
25 트렁크-**정이현** In the Trunk-**Jeong Yi-hyun**

남과 북 South and North

26 판문점-**이호철** Panmunjom-**Yi Ho-chol**
27 수난 이대-**하근찬** The Suffering of Two Generations-**Ha Geun-chan**
28 분지-**남정현** Land of Excrement-**Nam Jung-hyun**
29 봄 실상사-**정도상** Spring at Silsangsa Temple-**Jeong Do-sang**
30 은행나무 사랑-**김하기** Gingko Love-**Kim Ha-kee**

바이링궐 에디션 한국 대표 소설 set 3

서울 Seoul

31 눈사람 속의 검은 항아리-**김소진** The Dark Jar within the Snowman-**Kim So-jin**
32 오후, 가로지르다-**하성란** Traversing Afternoon-**Ha Seong-nan**
33 나는 봉천동에 산다-**조경란** I Live in Bongcheon-dong-**Jo Kyung-ran**
34 그렇습니까? 기린입니다-**박민규** Is That So? I'm A Giraffe-**Park Min-gyu**
35 성탄특선-**김애란** Christmas Specials-**Kim Ae-ran**

전통 Tradition

36 무자년의 가을 사흘-**서정인** Three Days of Autumn, 1948-**Su Jung-in**
37 유자소전-**이문구** A Brief Biography of Yuja-**Yi Mun-gu**
38 향기로운 우물 이야기-**박범신** The Fragrant Well-**Park Bum-shin**
39 월행-**송기원** A Journey under the Moonlight-**Song Ki-won**
40 협죽도 그늘 아래-**성석제** In the Shade of the Oleander-**Song Sok-ze**

아방가르드 Avant-garde

41 아겔다마-**박상륭** Akeldama-**Park Sang-ryoong**
42 내 영혼의 우물-**최인석** A Well in My Soul-**Choi In-seok**
43 당신에 대해서-**이인성** On You-**Yi In-seong**
44 회색 時-**배수아** Time In Gray-**Bae Su-ah**
45 브라운 부인-**정영문** Mrs. Brown-**Jung Young-moon**

바이링궐 에디션 한국 대표 소설 set 4

디아스포라 Diaspora

46 속옷-**김남일** Underwear-**Kim Nam-il**
47 상하이에 두고 온 사람들-**공선옥** People I Left in Shanghai-**Gong Sun-ok**
48 모두에게 복된 새해-**김연수** Happy New Year to Everyone-**Kim Yeon-su**
49 코끼리-**김재영** The Elephant-**Kim Jae-young**
50 먼지별-**이경** Dust Star-**Lee Kyung**

가족 Family

51 혜자의 눈꽃-**천승세** Hye-ja's Snow-Flowers-**Chun Seung-sei**
52 아베의 가족-**전상국** Ahbe's Family-**Jeon Sang-guk**
53 문 앞에서-**이동하** Outside the Door-**Lee Dong-ha**
54 그리고, 축제-**이혜경** And Then the Festival-**Lee Hye-kyung**
55 봄밤-**권여선** Spring Night-**Kwon Yeo-sun**

유머 Humor

56 오늘의 운세-**한창훈** Today's Fortune-**Han Chang-hoon**
57 새-**전성태** Bird-**Jeon Sung-tae**
58 밀수록 다시 가까워지는-**이기호** So Far, and Yet So Near-**Lee Ki-ho**
59 유리방패-**김중혁** The Glass Shield-**Kim Jung-hyuk**
60 전당포를 찾아서-**김종광** The Pawnshop Chase-**Kim Chong-kwang**